Just a Normal Tuesday

Kim Turrisi

KCP Loft

KCP Loft is an imprint of Kids Can Press

Text © 2017 Kim Turrisi

Kids Can Press gratefully acknowledges the financial support of the Government of Ontario, through the Ontario Media Development Corporation.

Published in Canada and the U.S. by Kids Can Press Ltd.
25 Dockside Drive, Toronto, ON M5A 0B5

Kids Can Press is a Corus Entertainment Inc. company

www.kidscanpress.com
www.kcploft.com

The text is set in Adobe Garamond Pro and Coal Hand Luke

Edited by Kate Egan
Cover and interior design by Michel Vrana
Cover image courtesy of iStock

Printed and bound in Altona, Manitoba, Canada, in 10/2016 by Friesens Corp.

CM 17 0 9 8 7 6 5 4 3 2 1

Library and Archives Canada Cataloguing in Publication

Turrisi, Kim, author
    Just a normal Tuesday / Kim Turrisi.

ISBN 978-1-77138-793-4 (hardback)

    I. Title.

PZ7.1.T87Ju 2017   j813'.6   C2016-902914-X

For my sister

Prologue

Today is such a Monday kind of Tuesday. It's blistering hot, I left my English paper on the dining room table, the Tater Tots — which are the only edible thing in the cafeteria — were gone by the time I got to lunch *and* Mrs. Lindley gave us a pop quiz in Algebra.

When my best friend, TJ, and I meet up after our last class, we do what we always do: dissect the day.

"Worst day. I got a C on a paper I was certain was a solid B. Then I got paired with John Lozano for a Biology project," he complains.

"Pop quiz that I know I tanked," I say, trying to one-up him because that's what we do.

"Not even close. I so win," he argues.

"I'll give this round to you. The Lozano factor pushed you over."

TJ and I land at the first bank of ugly drab metal lockers that cover the hallway walls of Parkland High School. I grab the dial of my locker without paying any attention: eleven to the right, seven to the left, eleven to the right again. It pops open with a familiar click. November 7 is my sister Jen's birthday. Easy to remember, plus they're my two lucky numbers. The vertical grayish-brown door swings open and hits the locker next to mine with a metal-on-metal ting.

The inside of my locker is decorated with photographs and postcards. My favorite is one of Jen and me standing in, yeah *in*, Westcott Fountain at Florida State when she graduated. It's a rite of passage for the seniors to jump in the fountain so I jumped in right along with her. We look nothing alike. Not our hair, not our body types. Nothing. Jen's curvy, I'm thinner. My hair is dark and hers is light brown.

"Maybe Mom had an affair with the FedEx guy," Jen says. It's her go-to explanation.

Six years my senior, Jen has always taken care of me and shielded me from any family discord. I was her baby when I was born. She traded Barbie and the other dolls in for yours truly. Her gregarious personality is bigger than life, and she's my biggest ally. She's Jennifer to my parents, Jen to her slew of friends and Jen Jen to me. When I was two and a half, she laughed at the way I said Jen, so I'd repeat it over and over to get her to smile.

It worked every time so it stuck.

A glossy postcard of the Eiffel Tower is taped sideways next to a picture of TJ and me holding a sign that says PARIS OR BUST in giant red letters. We're taking a gap year after graduation to backpack around Europe. Not that my parents know that yet. It isn't in their plan for me. Jen's on board though, and has a surefire plan to make it work.

As we walk toward Gertie, TJ's blue Jeep Wrangler, my green flip-flops stick to the hot blacktop.

"It's so fucking hot," I say, stating the obvious.

"Global fucking warming," TJ replies, pulling out his signature Blu electronic cigarette. He lights up and takes a long drag. I don't get the whole electronic-cigarette thing, but I have too much on my plate with this book report and our secret gap year plans, not to mention the SATs, to question his bad judgment. Besides, Thomas James McAndrews pretty much gets a pass for anything from me. We've been inseparable since I moved here over ten years ago. For just a split second we were boyfriend and girlfriend in middle school, until after a game of truth or dare gone awry, TJ realized he'd rather have his tongue in Jason Taylor's mouth than mine. His long, messy brown hair and gangly body make him a dead ringer for Jesus, depending on how the light hits him. The scar above his right eye is courtesy of his stepfather, who is one mean drunk.

TJ unlocks my door first and lets me hop in.

"McDonald's?" he asks, already knowing the answer. The Golden Arches is our place. I turn up the radio, the latest song by The National jams and we both sing along all the way to fast-food paradise with the promise of six fried nuggets and zesty barbecue dipping sauce on the horizon.

Today we opt for the drive-through window and take our food to go.

Then TJ turns to the elephant in the Jeep.

"Are we going to this end-of-the-year prom thing or what?" he asks. He can't really invite the person he wants to since that would require officially coming out and possible danger at home.

"We have to go for yearbook. It's the last big event before it goes to print."

"You know Chris's band is playing, right?"

Sophomore-year heartache stabs at me once more.

"I couldn't give a shit," I lie. I do give a lot of shits. I lost my virginity to Chris, a guy who whispered all the right things in my ear and managed to cloud my judgment with empty promises. I should have known better. Thankfully, I've managed to avoid him since the ugly incident.

"I'm wearing a powder-blue tux with black Vans. Totally retro," he says.

"Really?" I never know when he's joking.

"Rad, right?"

"Well, it doesn't exactly reinforce the straight thing." We come to a screeching halt at the end of my driveway.

"See you later? It's Taco Tuesday at Casa Azul," TJ says.

"I've got to write this paper. I just have to get it over with. Text me later," I say, grabbing the silver door handle.

"Come on, study break for tacos?"

"All right, all right. You win. How about seven-ish? That should give me time to crank this out."

"Peace out." He waves.

I watch him speed off as I saunter up the ornate driveway of my parents' dream house. They spent hours choosing pavers that would be covered by cars anyway. What was the point? My sister and I mock them all the time.

I hear Duke's incessant barking and can just picture him running in circles inside as I slide my key into the lock. Crap, I forgot to grab the mail. My dad is so OCD about the mail. Whoever gets home first has to get it immediately. Never know what could be in there, right? I mean, who wouldn't want to steal the discount pizza coupons and the endless catalogs? But my dad is Mr. Litigator so I've learned not to argue about things unless they really matter to me. I pick my battles. The mail isn't one of them.

Duke is still going nuts as I grab the mail from the custom oblong mailbox that mirrors the colors of the house. My father's pride and joy. He obsessed for days over the design of it. What he spent on that mailbox could feed a family of ten for at least a month. I tuck the stack of mail under my arm.

When I push the decorative hand-carved front door open, Duke greets me with sloppy kisses and muddy paws. Retriever-size paw prints decorate the Spanish-tile floor. Looks like he had a party for one in the backyard today. Mom will lose it when she sees holes in her prized garden. I ignore Duke's mess and head straight up to my room. I can't procrastinate any longer. I've gotta write this paper now if there's any hope of making it to Taco Tuesday.

I throw my books on top of my 1960s aluminum desk — the cardboard tucked tightly under one leg keeps it from wobbling — and move across my room toward the turntable. Vinyl is the only way to go.

Jen found this classic desk at a garage sale for like twenty bucks and said if I was going to be a writer, my desk had to mirror my style. Vintage, quirky, retro, that's me. The classic Rolling Stones *Tattoo You* album is just getting going. Perfect vibe. I toss the stack of mail and watch as it slides across the slippery surface of my desk. That's when I glimpse an envelope skidding out of the pile like it's stealing second base. The lettering on the envelope matches the postcards in my locker. Jen's writing. Odd that she'd send a letter but she does love to write.

I pick up the envelope and am immediately struck by the weight of it. Two stamps on the front. I'm ultra-careful not to rip it. Learned that the hard way when my grandparents sent money and I tore a crisp hundred-dollar bill. Jen knows I'm saving for my trip. Could she be sending some cold hard cash? That would be so like her. First thing I see is a note.

> My very bestest sister, Kai
> If you are reading this, I am already gone.

I scrutinize the stationery. It's definitely my sister's handwriting. Slanted, looping, like art. If there were an award for best cursive writing, Jen would bring home the hardware, hands down.

> I've watched you grow up since you were a baby.
> You've turned into an amazing person. I know you know
> how much I love you and have always wanted the best of
> everything for you. Please don't be disappointed in me for
> being too weak to face down my demons.

Demons? Disappointed? I snag my phone from my pocket and choose her number in my Favorites. Sometimes it's just easier to talk than read stuff that makes no sense. Like this.

Straight to voice mail. I return to the letter, curious.

That's when I see the word …

> funeral.

The gravity of that word knocks the wind out of me and, literally, my legs out from under me. I land on my bedroom floor with a thud.

I didn't set out to hurt you or Mom and Dad. I hope this doesn't cause you any embarrassment but there is no way out for me. I know this makes me a coward but I can't take the weight of things any longer.

"What the fuck are you talking about, Jen?" Through an onslaught of tears, I keep reading.

Mom understands you more than you think. Let her in. You can trust her. Please don't wear black to the funeral. Don't mourn me. Celebrate the wonderful life you have ahead of you.

This handwriting isn't art. Far from it. With each new paragraph, the letters are slanting down to the right and the words are bunched together, barely legible. A knife navigates its way from my gut to my sternum, filleting me, as I realize the magnitude of what's happening.

When she says *gone*, does she mean *dead*?

I leap toward the wastebasket. The vomit comes fast as my cries mix with anger. After I wipe my mouth off, I finish reading her last words to me.

This world is a terribly flawed place for someone like me. Don't ever let anyone change your outlook on life.

Get everything you can out of every minute and always work hard to get what you want. Everything I have is yours. It's not a lot but you'll have the car you've been asking for and some extra cash. Use it to get to Europe. If you don't go, you'll regret it. No looking back. Only forward.

It's like I'm caught in the current under a waterfall and can't find my way to the surface for air. I sound more like a wounded animal than a human being and tears stream from my eyes so fast they're blinding me.

Kai Bear, I don't expect you to understand this, but I'm not scared of death. The alternative is too painful. That pain is over now.
Please don't cry for me, I am finally at peace and pain free. You are strong, unlike me. Use every minute of your life doing what you love and loving what you do. Be happy. I will watch over you for the rest of your life and will always be in your corner.
Forgive me,
Jen Jen

I hear an earsplitting scream and realize it is coming from me. I breathe in and out, attempting to calm myself down. I refold the handwritten pages and it takes me four attempts to get them back in the envelope. This might be the last thing Jen will ever give me. Will ever say. The last. *The last?*

Chapter 1

I strain to focus on the situation at hand. Her apartment is less than twenty minutes away. There's a chance.

There just has to be.

Instinctively, I call TJ, my rock. Per usual, he picks up on the first ring: "Missed me, I see." When I hear his actual voice, I catch my breath for a moment.

"It's Jen. I think … I think …" I start wailing. "I think something horrible happened." I struggle to get out more. "I have to get to her. Please. I need you."

"Leaving now. Stay put, Kai, I'll be there in five."

I frantically hit my mom's number. It goes straight to voice mail. Fucking voice mail!

"Why can't you answer the phone, Mom? Just pick up the goddamn phone!" I screech. I hear the tone and I have to say something!

I steady my voice as best I can. "Mom, call me as soon as you get this."

I hang up and attempt to reach my dad. Same thing. "Daddy, call me," I say. I haven't called him Daddy for at least five years.

I bump the desk and the rest of the mail drops to the floor, raining bills and two more letters with handwriting that is all too familiar: one addressed to Marie Sheehan, the other to John Sheehan. My parents.

Jesus Christ.

I race down the stairs and wait in the driveway for TJ. I try to reach both of my missing parents again, just in case.

"Something terrible has happened, you have to call me. Now!!" I scream. Do I need to send up a flare? I start to text them just as TJ is skidding into the driveway. He jumps out of his Jeep and I rush into his waiting arms.

"What happened, Kai?"

I'm on that razor's edge of believing she might still be alive and knowing the truth is she could be dead. I steel myself to say something I never dreamed I'd ever have to say to my best friend. Waterworks take over and I have no control over the ache that is squeezing my heart. "I think Jen killed herself. I don't even know when. I just saw her on Sunday. We have to get there. Maybe she's still alive. I don't know."

He turns ashen. TJ holds me so close that I can smell the distinct odor of his soap. Eucalyptus.

"What do you even mean 'killed herself'?" he asks.

"She sent me a letter. Said she had demons. She couldn't take it anymore. I don't know, TJ. Please, we have to go to her. I can't find my fucking parents anywhere." I know I'm not making any sense but none of this makes sense.

TJ steadies me, helping me into the passenger seat, reaching across my lap to buckle me in. He looks at me with sad dark eyes that are welling up. "I think we should call the police or 911."

I nod and punch three digits on my phone.

"I'll take side streets, I know a shortcut," he says as he navigates his way down streets I didn't know existed.

The 911 operator answers and I jump right in. "It's my sister. She might be dead. Please help me."

"Miss, I need your name. Where are you?" an ultra-calm voice says.

"Kai Sheehan. In a car. Going to my sister's apartment. There was a letter from her when I got home from school. My parents ... I don't know ... Please."

"What's the address?" she continues, keeping her composure.

"I can't think. Please," I whimper. *Please* is on repeat in my head. Like, *Please do not let this be happening. Please.*

"I'll stay on the phone with you. Try your best to remember," she encourages me without being too pushy.

"It's 2421 Ocean View Terrace, apartment number 2," I manage. TJ rubs my back with the hand that isn't steering us through the side streets of Fort Lauderdale.

"I've dispatched an ambulance and the police. They'll probably get there before you arrive. Are your parents with you?" she asks.

"I can't reach them. No one is answering their phones," I sob.

"I'll stay right here with you," the stranger on the other end reassures me.

All I can do is pray silently to a God I don't really believe in.

"Is this really happening?" I ask, hoping the answer is no. I just can't go to that place yet.

TJ reaches for me, gently drawing my head to his shoulder.

"I'm so sorry, Kai. I don't know what to say." I feel his tears spill onto my cheek.

We ride in penetrating silence until the moment TJ wheels into my sister's art deco apartment complex. There is a sea of flashing red lights and a twisted maze of police cars, a lone black car and an ambulance. They line the road inside the secluded complex. Tucked away in a cul-de-sac, the fifteen units encircling the pool were built in the 1940s. It had the charm and privacy that Jen craved.

"Oh my God," I say.

TJ takes charge of the 911 operator. "Ma'am, thanks for staying on with us. We're here, so are the police and everybody else." I snatch the phone from his hands once the operator hangs up. I have to get to Jen.

So many lights.

So many people.

The vehicles are all parked haphazardly in the middle of the street outside the busted-in door of Jen's tiny one-bedroom place. No order whatsoever. Car doors left wide open. I leap out of the Jeep before it rolls to a complete stop. I'm blinded by the need to get to my sister and help her. My legs start running and one of the police officers stops me with his extended forearm. I struggle to get away.

"My sister is in there!" I yell. I shove and flail. I have to get to her.

"Your parents are on the way," he offers.

"How? What?" Nothing is computing.

"We found your father's office number in her phone. It was on her nightstand. I'm so sorry," I hear him say through the fog that has rolled into my head.

TJ sprints toward me but not before I break free from the police officer's arms.

I rush through my sister's living room, dodging the ottoman, blowing by her oversize leather chair, passing through throngs of uniformed officers, into her bedroom.

Then everything stops.

Chapter 2

Time stands still.

There she is, smack in front of me, my beautiful sister lounging in her king-size bed, wearing her favorite worn plaid pajama bottoms and Florida State *Fear the Spear* T-shirt.

She's surrounded by pillows in various shades of purple, her favorite color. Purple everything.

I notice a notepad, the one she must have used to write my letter, right next to a book of stamps and an endless pile of family photographs. She looks so peaceful, like she's crashed out. It reminds me of all our sleepovers. We'd give each other mani-pedis, we'd order Hawaiian pizza with jalapeños and she'd counsel me on our parents. They don't really get me. She's going to run interference when I tell them about my gap year.

Was going to.

My eye catches the photo frame of Duke's paw print I made for her a few birthdays back. It took me almost an hour to get him to sit still for that.

"She was already gone when we got here," a voice near me says, snapping me out of what used to be.

I slam back into my body.

There's extreme pain, like a four-alarm fire, raging inside my chest. My sister isn't surrounded by nail polish or a pizza box. Instead, a wineglass lies on its side.

Dead like her.

Empty pill bottles pepper the nightstand, right next to her dog-eared copy of *On the Road* by Jack Kerouac. I flick off a hand that tries to stop me from getting to her side. "She's my fucking sister, get away from me." Some demon inside just hisses at the poor guy in my path to Jen. I bodycheck him to get to her. No one else makes the mistake of trying to stop me.

I need to hold her, touch her. One more time. But I freeze, stuck to the muted purple-and-gray area rug next to her bed.

I drop to my knees, swallow hard and take her hand in mine. It's so cold, like gripping an ice cube. So still. I reach for the blanket neatly folded at the foot of the bed to cover her hand and mine.

I shift closer to her bedside table, my eyes on the pill bottles. Lots of colors, names. Where did these come from? She never went to the doctor.

Like, never.

It was Eastern medicine for her all the way, homeopathic everything. Until this. Making sense of the senseless.

The dark-rinse blue jeans and rumpled shirt she wore two short days ago, only forty-eight hours, lie in a heap where she must have left them after Sunday dinner at our house.

I grab the soft chambray shirt from the floor, drawing it close to my face to breathe in her scent. Kiehl's Musk, her signature smell. I wrap the shirt around me tightly, wishing her arms were in the empty sleeves, holding me. Soothing me. My whole body is shaking.

I can't stop staring at her face. Her soft, light chestnut hair, lying delicately around her face. The long eyelashes that never needed mascara. A lone beauty mark on her right cheek, small but noticeable in a movie star kind of way. A light blue tint taking over her usual fair skin.

What if I forget what she looks like?

A torrent follows, forcing me to drop my forehead on the edge of the bed. "Miss," a voice whispers, "I think you should come into the living room and wait for your parents."

I have to talk to Jen. I lean closer to her ear and ask, "How could you do this? I don't understand."

Then I force myself to back away though the last thing I want to do is to leave her.

In the living room of her tiny apartment, everything looks precisely the same as when I last visited her for our monthly movie date. The chocolate-colored Restoration Hardware chenille throw Mom bought her as a housewarming gift draped at the end of her couch. The June issue of *Rolling Stone* magazine with "Top Ten Summer Concerts" on the cover, black Sharpie circling Ed Sheeran. Jen's iPad tossed next to her distressed-leather backpack.

I vaguely hear the drone of familiar voices and whip around to see my parents in conversation with the police officer who tried to stop me when I first walked in. My dad's Windsor knot is cockeyed, his face pale, radiating heartbreak. My mother's agony runs a marathon down her face.

20

"Where's my daughter?" my father says, his worried eyes scanning the room as he rushes through the uniforms to my side. "Oh, Kai." He reels me in close. When my father's salty tears land on my face, I realize it's the first time in my life I've ever seen him show any emotion at all, let alone cry.

Over my father's shoulder, I see my mother collapse, inconsolable as her worst fear is confirmed by a stranger in a dark blue uniform. Paramedics rush to her aid, handing her water and tissues. I could stand to replace the liquids that have left my body in the last half hour. "No! No! No!" My mom keeps repeating that over and over. I was stuck on repeat with *please*, she's stuck on *no*.

Suddenly I want to be let loose. I jerk back away from my father's embrace. "What took you so long?" I snap at him. "I left you a bunch of messages, you never called me back."

Dad grimaces, sniffling. "Oh, Kai, I never got to them. I'm so sorry. I hurried over here as soon as the police called my office. I picked your mom up on the way. All they said was there'd been an accident and we rushed right here and … and …" He stops. It doesn't matter anyway.

"It wasn't an accident," I mutter.

I try to focus.

"She wrote to me — to all of us — about what she had done, what she was doing. I called 911. It happened so fast. TJ drove me. I got here as soon as I could but I was too late. I couldn't save her." I know I'm rambling but, God, I've just seen my only sister's lifeless body with my own shattered eyes. My mom makes her way to us just as I get out the only words that really matter.

"She killed herself."

Those three words shake me to my core.

"It was an accident," Mom says. "They said there was an accident."

She keeps insisting.

"An accident, Kai."

"They lied," I tell her. I mean, I just say it flat out.

The misery on my mother's face is palpable. I hate the words as I'm saying them. I start to cry softly but march on. I have to. It's on me. Jen put it all on me. Christ.

"Suicide, Mom."

She reaches for my dad.

"In my letter. She said she couldn't take the pain anymore. I don't understand. Everything was okay on Sunday, wasn't it?"

"I thought so." I barely recognize the slight voice that's coming out of my mom's mouth. Her shoulders start to shudder; she's whimpering like a child.

"Mr. Sheehan," a man in a suit with a badge on his belt interrupts, "Detective Daly." He shakes my dad's hand. "I'm sorry, we'll have to ask you a few questions. Just routine paperwork."

Nothing is routine about a twenty-two-year-old killing herself on a random Tuesday.

Mom and I hang on to each other like we're clinging on for dear life while my father answers questions that no longer matter.

"What was your daughter's full name, sir?"

"Jennifer Leigh Sheehan."

"How old was she, sir?"

"Twenty-two." That crushes me once more. My dad's sheet-white skin accents the black stubble on his cheeks. Random thoughts keep popping into my head. We were supposed to learn how to surf. We have tickets to the Fleetwood Mac reunion concert in Orlando at the end of the summer, our entire road trip planned. Jen used to play "Landslide" on her guitar to lull me to sleep when I was six. I still listen to it when I have insomnia. She was supposed to move me into my dorm at Florida State after my gap year; she wouldn't even entertain the idea of me not being a Seminole. I was going to be her maid of honor someday.

She was supposed to *be here*.

"Sir, the paramedics think she's been dead for some time. When was the last time you saw Jennifer?"

"Jen," I correct him. It seems important.

"Sunday. At dinner," Dad says.

"We had spaghetti and meatballs," I say. Not that it matters.

He scribbles the unimportant information on a small notepad. I edge closer to my father.

"Sir, I have to ask, is there anyone who might want to hurt your daughter?"

I step up. "She killed herself."

Detective Daly stops writing, turning all his attention in my direction.

I continue, "She wrote letters. I got mine when I came home from school."

The agony that traces my mom's face stabs at me.

"Thank you. I'm so very sorry for your loss," he says. He runs his hand through his hair and turns to my dad. "Those are all the questions I have. The medical examiner is here for your daughter's body."

"Medical examiner?" my dad asks.

"We have to dispatch them for anything that might be a homicide, but since she left a suicide note, there's no need for an autopsy. Unless you'd like one."

I can't hold back. "No one is cutting my sister." Jesus Christ.

The detective powers on. It's all part of the routine. "They can coordinate with the funeral home. Who would you like them to call?"

You could almost hear a pin drop. My dad's face is blank, glazed over. My mom and I are on mute.

Officer Daly turns to my father. "Sir?"

"I have no idea." John Sheehan always has the answers. He is the master of the courtroom, never at a loss for words. His ability to make truth out of words is his moneymaker.

Just not today.

"I want to see my daughter," he says with an anguished crack in his voice.

"I'll take you back to her," Detective Daly states.

Dad reaches for Mom's hand, gently placing it in his, their fingers twining together. They move toward Jen's room at the pace of molasses. I fall back on the tapestry ottoman that once resided in my grandma Sheehan's condo and cradle one of the throw pillows to my chest; I just can't go back to her bedroom and see them see her.

I silently wish I had some weed or maybe a shooter of vodka. Actually, a handle of vodka is more like it. Anything to dull the throbbing in my head.

TJ and I began a weekend diet of both after my ugly breakup sophomore year and it became part of our routine. If Jen knew, she would have killed me. The beers we shared were fine, the rest she would not have approved of. At all.

So ironic.

I start to text Emily, my closest girlfriend — her family lives five McMansions down from us. Then I realize this is one of those god-awful moments you are forced to say words out loud. I can't send a text. I'm going to have to call.

As soon as she answers, my eyes well up and I stumble over my words. "Jen's gone." That's all I manage to say, two words. One of the milling police officers offers me some water, not vodka, and I chug it, almost choking. I hear Emily calling for her mom, who takes the phone from her.

"Kai, what's happened? Emily said Jen's gone. Gone where?"

She's not getting it either.

"She died, Mrs. Lancaster." That makes six times already that I've told that to someone. TJ, the 911 operator, my two parents, now my second family, Emily and her mom. I could go a lifetime without ever uttering those words again. Mrs. Lancaster starts to weep.

"Oh my God, what happened?"

"She's … just … I can't … dead." Nothing makes sense. Not Jen dying or the words I attempt.

Mrs. Lancaster says something about bringing food. As if anyone wants to eat.

"Okay." There's really no other response. I hang up and return to my parents.

My mother, father and I reluctantly leave the professionals to do what they do best: clean up someone's mess. Though no one will ever be able to fix this one.

I whip my aviator sunglasses out of my purse before we head outside, my eyes feeling swollen and surely bloodred. The ache in my heart consumes every inch of me. The humidity of the early Florida evening fogs up my lenses and I don't bother wiping them off. The last thing I need is a clearer picture of what's in front of me.

When my mother takes a startled breath, I slide the sunglasses down my nose just enough to see what she's looking at. A stretcher is being hauled out of a stark white vehicle. A hearse? No. I see the words MEDICAL EXAMINER in bold blue letters. A woman with a badge affixed to her shirt pocket removes a black body bag from the back, and catches me staring. I manage to clear the lump that's settled in my throat.

"Please don't zip her in that bag," I say. Not Jen. "She's claustrophobic."

The medical examiner pushes the bag aside, her face drawn with sorrow. "I'm so sorry for your loss." Her voice reminds me of my sister's.

I glance over at my mother, who's wiping away her distress. One of her diamond droplet earrings has been lost in the melee. Along with one daughter.

We are silent in the car. Mom pops a tiny orange pill into her mouth. I glance over my shoulder and watch my sister's apartment disappear through my tears.

Chapter 3

The second we get home we all retreat to our separate corners of the house. The mound of mail is on my desk exactly where I left it, and I know what I have to do next whether I like it or not. There's no easy way out of this. One letter open, two still sealed.

Again, it's on me.

I trudge into the steel-and-granite kitchen, finding my mom at the breakfast island, hunched over a picture of our former family. She hasn't bothered to reapply her makeup, and my mother is always, I mean always, on point with her image. Lawn signs with her face decorate some of the wealthiest streets in the Fort Lauderdale Beach area. Sheehan Realty, Mom's thriving business, was built on her reputation and appearance. "I don't know what happened," Mom says. "She was fine on Sunday when she was here for dinner. It was all so sudden. What if it was an accidental overdose?"

A convenient tsunami of Catholic denial just sucked in the entire McMansion, dog and all. She doesn't even sound like she remotely believes her own words as they tumble out of her mouth. Still, I can't listen to her lie this away. "Give me a break, Mom."

I plow on through.

"You saw all the pill bottles, the empty wineglass? And she sent me a letter, Mom. She sent you one, too." I show it to her. "In mine, she killed herself. She wasn't at some party mixing Jack Daniel's and Molly. She sat alone in her apartment, wrote us all goodbye letters and ended her life. On purpose."

The sting of my words is written all over my mom's fatigued face. But I am pissed.

"Please stop saying that," she pleads.

"She was worried we would be embarrassed. I can't believe she thought that. You aren't, are you?"

Her hesitation answers me. I can't even look at her. I set the letter down next to her glass of vodka, no ice, and wonder if she'd notice me pouring a drink for myself. "Are you going to read it?" I ask.

"I'd like to read it alone," she replies, void of emotion.

With the final letter to deliver, I find Dad tucked inside our tech-heavy family room — complete with two flat-screen TVs on the wall so Dad and his buddies can watch two games at once — draped over the wrought-iron-and-marble bar he bought in Italy on a business trip. He's pouring three fingers of Johnnie Walker Blue into a crystal cocktail glass with one oversize cube of ice. He takes a long pull from it, then plants himself in his leather recliner, cradling the scotch glass like it's a baby.

I offer him the envelope and explain, though I doubt this needs an explanation. "I picked up the mail like you asked us to do. First one home gets the mail. Jen sent each one of us a letter. One for me, one for you, one for Mom. I only read mine. Here's yours."

I thrust it into his hand.

He stares at it but can't look at me. Or maybe it's just that he won't. I wish he would just open it. Right here, in front of me. Instead, he grips it tightly in his left hand, draining the scotch in his right.

"Dad?" I know I sound small. "I need to know more. Maybe your letter will explain." Sharing is not a Sheehan trait.

"I can't, Kai."

We're the perfect family, always the life of the party at any public event. But once those double doors slam shut, so do the feelings.

First phone calls, now letters. I'm the messenger of death. Defeated, I shuffle into the dining room, retreating to the home of my sister's chair. I'm hanging on to anything and everything Jen. The Sheehans sit in the same chairs for every meal, always have. Dad and Mom at the two ends of the table. Me across from my sister. Just close enough that we can kick each other under the table and roll our eyes about our parents. Now what do we do with her spot at the table?

I feel the weight of Duke's face on my knee nuzzling me. Jen found him secured to a post with no tags or collar, just a note nearby that said *Free*, while she was jogging along a trail in Birch State Park early one Sunday morning a few years back and couldn't bring herself to take him to a shelter. The white heart-shaped markings on his chest sucked her in, so she said. But his earnest brown eyes did it for me. Our father wasn't a big fan of Jen's I-can-save-the-world lifestyle but it's who she was. And no one says no to a dog.

Not even my dad.

Jen was heartbroken when she couldn't take him to her new apartment with its strict no-pets policy, but I think my father was thrilled with the rule. That way he had Duke all to himself. That dog stole my dad's heart.

"It's been a shitty day, buddy," I explain, scratching the top of his cashmere-soft head. "The suckiest of suck." Familiar drops gush down my face. He nudges me with his snout, and I just know he understands, he feels the shift in the house. His food is still sitting in his bowl untouched. His world has changed along with ours, and his eyes beg me for answers. "I got nothing but I will. Trust me." He licks my hand to show his faith in me.

I send a text to TJ.

You disappeared. I wish I could. Xo

He responds immediately, like he does.

Didn't want to be in the way. How r u?

Numb.

Need anything?

Just my sister.

When I walk back into the family room, Dad is staring at his lap, now rubbing the folded letter like it's a genie in a bottle. Like somehow he's gonna get three wishes if he rubs it just so. He appears to have aged ten years since I handed him the envelope. At least I know he opened it, the flap tells me so. His pin-striped suit jacket and solid blue tie lie in a heap on the floor next to his unopened briefcase.

"Did you know she was so unhappy that she would do something like this?" I ask, almost afraid of the answer.

"I had no idea. When we had lunch last week, she was just Jen. She kept talking about the fundraiser she was helping to organize for the ASPCA. She even brought the press release she wrote to show me. She was so proud of it. She joked about coming home with another dog." His voice cracks.

Jen has always been the free-spirit do-gooder, unlike me. In high school, when she wasn't volunteering at the food bank, she walked dogs at the shelter every Saturday. If that wasn't enough, every month she organized a group of teens to pick up litter on the beach. I'm more of a sleep-until-noon girl. She made it her mission to change that about me.

It's not working yet.

"How could we not have known? How is that even possible, Dad?"

His head drops. "I can't."

I will myself to speak through the fresh flood pouring over my cheeks, feeling like I'm breathing under water with my mouth open. Instead, I race upstairs to my room, slamming my door and shutting the world out. Stretched out on my bed, head cradled by my pillow, phone raised in the air over my face, I scroll back through the texts between me and my sister. The first few were from Sunday night after she went home. Had to be after midnight.

Glad you came to dinner, Jen. Mom and Dad won't get off the college application thing. You aced the distraction plan. Time for the next step. Gap year, here I come.

Her response almost makes me laugh.

Almost.

You know I have their number. I got you. Love you little sis.
You too.

I freeze on the next text, her last to me ever.

Never forget that xo

She knew right that second with each letter she tapped that it would be her last text to me. Fuck.

Instinctively, I pick up Hershel, the cotton-candy-pink stuffed monkey that Jen bought me for my sixth birthday, and squeeze him tightly, crying for what will never be. She told me he would keep me company when she wasn't around. I hope this wasn't what she had in mind. I ponder what must have happened after she sent me that last text on Sunday. It makes me sick, but I go there. She made herself comfortable on her bed, then methodically began popping pills one after another as she perused family photos.

Blue.

Orange.

White.

A chaser of Cabernet after each one just for good measure, making sure she closed the deal.

Then she scribbled a goodbye letter to each of us, meticulously sealing each one before walking them out to the bank of mailboxes next to the pool. Back in her bed, she slowly drifted into a sleep she would never wake up from. Judging by all those empty bottles, she took enough pills to tranquilize an elephant.

Opening my laptop, I click iTunes and select a song that really captures the spirit of this day. Cole Swindell, "You Should Be Here." Turning it up, I feel the lyrics hard as I hunt through the photo stream on my iPhone, pausing on every picture, searching her eyes for signs of depression. I burst out in hysterics when I see Jen and me outside the American Airlines Arena pointing to a sign emblazoned with ONE DIRECTION. My first concert. When she told me she would take me to see anyone I wanted, I bet she wasn't counting on that. I'm sure her ears were bleeding the entire time, but she never let on.

I hear Cole belt out the chorus and all I can think is, "You should be here, Jen," but you're not.

I thought I was all cried out.

I'm not.

There's another pic of Jen and me drinking bottles of Bud Light Lime on the beach during her spring break two years ago. My first beer. Mom and Dad would shit if they saw this. I wore her down after weeks of begging when I turned fourteen.

Determined to find a clue, I keep looking.

There's a picture of her at Disney World, taken a few weeks after she got home from Europe. One of the last family trips we'd ever take. She's wearing pink chinos with a crease, a striped tank top, flip-flops and mouse ears, posing with Winnie-the-Pooh and Tigger. A happy-go-lucky smile is plastered all over her face.

Nothing. Not a clue.

Dying is black and white, but suicide is gray.

* * *

I'm standing in a corner downstairs, watching an endless stream of cupcakes and casseroles arriving with half the neighborhood. Obviously, they've cleared out the prepared-food case at Publix. Hope no one else in Fort Lauderdale wants a precooked lasagna tonight.

I swear I've never met half of these people. Their eyes are brimming with compassion and sorrow.

I nod at the *I'm so sorrys* and promises of *We are here if you need anything*, but it's all so absurd. My sister kills herself and it's suddenly raining food.

After a thousand years, I spot friendly faces hugging my parents. We lock eyes. I point to the stairs and we all slink up to my room unnoticed. I have never been so happy to see Emily and TJ. Plus they are bearing gifts: a pint of Fireball, several bags of Kettle Chips and Cheetos and some weed. Nothing screams *brain numbing* like a shot or two of 33-percent-alcohol cinnamon whiskey.

TJ nearly pulls me to the floor with the weight of his grip on me. "I loved your sister, Kai."

"She loved you, too." I didn't know it was possible, but I am almost dried out.

"I just don't get it, am I blind? How did this happen? What did I miss?"

"Oh, Kai. This is so fucked up." Emily embraces me, her athletic body nearly crushing mine, her cocoa skin warm against my miserable face. My stomach stops flipping momentarily with her tender touch. She's what I imagine a Zen master would be.

"Like, she chose this. So not fucking fair," I choke.

TJ unscrews the top of the Fireball bottle and passes it to me. I guide the bottle to my lips, and my mouth flames up with first contact and it burns like hell going down. At least I feel something other than agony.

As the inferno of burning liquid erupts in my belly, I'm struck by the obvious. "Life is so fragile."

"More than we all know," TJ adds.

I turn to the plethora of photos and postcards that decorate the elaborate picture-frame headboard over my bed. My sister went through a do-it-yourself phase and we made it together two years ago. A bonding activity is what she called it. We did a lot of those. She vowed to fill it and made good on her promise once she began to see the world.

Dabbing my eyes with my T-shirt, I freeze on each one of them.

Jen insisted on writing letters and postcards every other week during the year she was gone. The ones currently pinned on my headboard are stand-out favorites for one reason or another. Some for the actual picture on the postcard, some for what she wrote on the back. An English Lit minor, she was quite big on the written word. When she came back from Europe, I missed the postcards.

"She couldn't wait for us to visit all the places she went," I say to TJ, unpinning a postcard from Bellagio, Italy.

Bellagio is one of the small towns on Lake Como. Wait till you see what I'm bringing you back from here, little sis. Xo

Eyeballing the picture-perfect handwriting comforts me, if just for a moment. Emily points to a quote in the middle of the headboard. "I love that one," she says. "Jack Kerouac."

"Me, too. They both loved the adventure of it all."

"You'll always have these," TJ reminds me as he hands me the Fireball.

"How could this person" — I point at the headboard, then continue — "choose death? It doesn't add up."

I hear the distinctive click of my mother's Louboutin heels coming up the stairs, hitting every hardwood step along the way. *Click. Click. Click.*

"Shit." I quickly screw the top on the contraband and hide it under my pillow.

She knocks just loud enough to hear. Even her hand is worn out.

"Come in," I say.

Mom pokes her head in. "Emily, your parents are getting ready to head home."

Emily stands up to leave, straightening her cotton flowery skirt, leaning in to kiss my wet cheek. TJ takes my hand, his leather bracelets brushing my flesh.

"I should get going, too, so you can get some sleep. Or do you want me to stay until you fall asleep? Because I totally can."

"No, it's okay. I kind of just want to stare at a wall and hope my mind goes blank."

He squeezes my hand. "Whatever you want. I'll come by after class tomorrow," he says. "Text me if you need me, though. No matter what time it is."

All I can scare up is a weak nod.

By eleven o'clock everyone who's invaded our space has long gone, leaving a wake of nine-by-eleven cheese-topped pans and endless baked goods. The sight of it makes me gag.

Rotating the nozzle, I let the water in my shower heat up. I undress, letting the day's clothing fall in a pile, except for the chambray shirt. I draw it up to my face and drink in the scent of the past, then place it neatly next to the garnet-and-gold boxers I got the last time we visited Jen at Florida State just before graduation.

It feels like a lifetime ago.

Stepping into the shower, I let the steam suck me in. I let the scalding-hot water fall over me, washing away the ugliness of this not-so-ordinary Tuesday.

Only nothing can wash it away.

Chapter 4

The morning brings more darkness. As soon as I open my eyes, I reach for my phone to text my sister. We hardly missed a single morning since she left for college, yet no texts on Monday or Tuesday. I should have known something was off.

I stare at my phone screen.

Years of comforting words that connected us.

Now, nothing.

My eye catches the handblown Christmas ornament Jen brought me back from Italy. An emerald-colored tree with teeny multicolored ornaments melted into the center of it. Christmas was our favorite holiday. I keep it out year-round. Jen said it would bring me luck.

What would be lucky is if this was just a nightmare and today wasn't Wednesday, the day after.

Walking downstairs, the first thing I see is *the chair* in the dining room. Hers. My eyes start to leak.

I notice an overflowing platter of cheese eggs and toast on the breakfast bar.

"Are you hungry? I made all your favorites." What she means is all of my and Jen's favorites. We both love breakfast any time of day. *Loved*. I hate the past tense already.

My stomach turns at the sight of food. It looks disgusting but I don't want to hurt Mom's feelings. "Not right now, thanks."

I grab a Starbucks Sumatra K-Cup and gently glide it into the Keurig. Usually, I'm a decaf-with-lots-of-creamer girl. Today seems like a good time to add caffeine. I got about two hours of sleep last night. Every time I closed my eyes, I saw Jen.

"Father Michael can do the mass on Saturday morning. Do we want a wake on Friday?" Mom asks Dad.

"No." I answer for him. "She wouldn't want two days of mourning. Ever. What the hell is wrong with you?" This little outburst gives my parents pause.

"Honey ..." My mom starts down a road I'm not traveling.

"Mom, don't you remember when Grandpa died and you made us go to the wake *and* the funeral? She hated every second of it." I'm not budging on this.

"It's what Catholics do," she says.

"Oh my God. We aren't even close to Catholic. I'm begging you not to make this an event. I cannot handle more than one day of this misery and I'm not even sure about that. It's such a barbaric ritual. Please."

There's that word again.

"We have to go to the funeral home this morning to finalize the arrangements and pick out a casket," Dad says a bit too matter-of-factly for my liking.

I snap at him. "Casket?"

"It has to be done, Kai."

"Today?" I yelp.

"It's part of it, sweetie," Denial Mom says, flipping pancakes.

My weary eyes constantly refill. "She just died." I'm coming unhinged and don't even bother to try to stop myself. I don't want to.

"Why does everything have to be finalized right this damn second? It's not going away just because you want it to. She's gone, as in never coming back." It's like they just want to move through the what-to-do-when-someone-dies checklist like it's a competition and they have to win.

"That's enough, Kai," Dad casually remarks, never looking up from the paper. He finishes the last sip of his brew. "I'll take Duke for a walk, then we can head over to the funeral home. I made the appointment for nine thirty."

"You don't have to go with us," Mom says, turning away from the skillet and toward me.

The last thing in the world I want to do is pick out a casket for my sister. But I have to do it. I really have to do it. I slam down my coffee cup. "I'm still here. I'm part of this family."

Dad leaves and I hear the sound of Duke's leash clang against his tag followed by happy barking. I'll never have that feeling of free and easy ever again. I wish I was a dog. Anything other than what I am.

An only child.

I try one more time. "Mom. Please. It's important. I'm not ready."

Seeing my anguish, she relents. "We can move the appointment back an hour, Kai. But we can't put it off forever. Have some breakfast. You need to eat before we leave."

Mom goes upstairs, leaving me alone. Loneliness swallows me. It's so still and quiet. I need to hear the sound of my sister's voice telling me that it's going to be okay.

* * *

Funeral homes have a distinct smell. Disinfectant on crack.

Probably to mask the scent of death.

A death vibe permeates the stark white walls, the short-pile pallid gray carpet, the whole damn place. It all reeks of the grim reaper. The lighting has a golden hue, presumably to mask the pallor of the pained faces grieving their loved ones. Boxes of white Kleenex are on hand every few feet. Barnes and Sons Funeral Home has been part of the landscape of Fort Lauderdale since the early 1900s and remains the go-to for any and all local funeral needs: so noted my mom on the mostly silent drive over. Even the soft music playing from the ceiling speakers screams death. Every step we take is bringing us closer to the end.

My parents and I sit quietly, properly, on a flower-print couch in the reception area. God, it looks just like Grandma's condo. There are mahogany tables and chairs that match the couch, with little white doilies on the armrests. Jen and I used to rearrange Grandma's whenever we visited growing up. I fixate on a small glass dish that is overflowing with red-and-white mints like the ones at the hostess station of every family-style restaurant in the country. For some reason, they're Jen's favorite.

My mind wanders back to the letters. Jen's suicide notes. I hate thinking of those words. We've yet to discuss the contents of our letters though I'm certain we've all read them. Mom's is tucked in her purse without the envelope. Dad's hasn't moved from the arm of his recliner.

I've managed to chew all the skin off my right thumb knuckle just since we arrived. I wipe away the blood on my rumpled Junk Food Orange Crush T-shirt, careful not to get any on Jen's chambray shirt, which I'm wearing over it. The last shirt she wore. Mom leans over. "You really could have dressed up a bit more. The T-shirt?"

"I have on closed-toe shoes, that's dressed up for me," I reply.

"Jesus Christ, Kai." That's the best she can muster up. Even she knows she's being ridiculous right now.

"Is she back there?" I ask. I know it sounds bizarre, but I find it comforting. She's still above ground with us. I can't even think about what comes next.

"Yes," Dad says solemnly, staring down at his wingtips.

"I hope she's not cold." She loved the beach, the sunshine. Tears snake their way along my face and drip onto my jeans. "It's freezing in here."

For the bodies, I suppose. That makes sense. Jen alone in some freezer, like a box of Popsicles, does not. My mom reaches for my hand and pats it.

"Good morning. Sam Barnes." A gentleman with salt-and-pepper hair, wearing a funeral-black suit and a starched white shirt, extends his hand. Dad gets up to shake it. The pity in Mr. Barnes's eyes drills through my body. Does he dress like this for everyone or is this reserved for the most extreme tragedies? A suicide suit. It gets more absurd with each passing minute.

"John Sheehan. This is my wife, Marie, and our daughter Kai."

My father's tone is flat and studied like he's meeting a client for the first time.

"I'm so very sorry for your loss," Mr. Barnes says.

Not as sorry as I am, I think. He never even met my sister. All the niceties make me sick. Mr. Barnes leads us into his office. The Kleenex boxes and mints are multiplying like rabbits. "I've spoken to the priest and understand that he'll be officiating the mass at St. Patrick's."

"What? How do I get on the family email distribution list?" I snap.

"Kai, please." Mom jumps down my throat.

"Mass? You have got to be kidding me." I keep pounding.

"It's what she wanted."

"She has a name. And when did *she* say that?"

"Not now," Dad growls.

Hell if I'm backing down on this. "I want to know."

Mom pinches the fatty part of my arm like she used to do in church when I had a tantrum. I refuse to make a sound even though it hurts like hell. She murmurs, "My letter stated her wishes. She was clear so we're doing it."

That zips my trap. But when did Jen become religious? We haven't gone to St. Patrick's for years unless you count Christmas Eve and an occasional Easter.

"I'm sorry, Mr. Barnes, this has been difficult for all of us," Mom apologizes.

"Difficult? That's the understatement of the century." My world has turned upside down and they're acting so polite. So ordinary. So fake.

"Can you please calm down?"

"Don't tell me to calm down, my sister is dead!" I shout. I just

43

completely lose it. I am myself and a shrieking maniac all at the same time.

Mr. Barnes says this is part of it, it's perfectly all right. Yes, now the funeral director is weighing in on my behavior.

My mother takes my shoulders with her hands. "Kai, let's just agree to get through this as best we can." There's a note of desperation in her voice that I totally understand.

I won't meet anybody's eyes.

"I just miss her," I squeak.

"We all do," Dad says earnestly. "But we have to do this."

I bite back another wave of anger because he's right. No one is serving up any alternatives. The end.

"The caskets are in the back room. We can go there now and have a look," Mr. Barnes continues in his monotone voice.

"Kai, you can wait here if you'd like," Dad offers, softer.

But I don't trust them to make the right decision.

There's something eerie about walking into a room filled wall to wall with caskets, and suddenly I have the nervous giggles. You know when the fear is too much to endure? Mom clears her throat, and Dad raises his eyebrows in my direction. The two of them amble over to a dark cherrywood coffin that reminds me of the one my grandpa Sheehan was buried in two years ago.

"Totally wrong" drops out of my mouth.

"I'm happy to answer any questions," offers Mr. Barnes.

"What's the difference between them?" Mom's face is stiff, like she's trying not to break down.

"The standard casket is made of the thinnest metal, a twenty gauge. The interior is a very thin crepe with no padding," Mr. Barnes fires off. Then on cue: "To be completely transparent with you, the standard casket does not have a rubber gasket to seal from outside elements."

My father jumps in quickly. "We don't want that one."

Mr. Barnes points at another option with a lot more enthusiasm. "This one is stainless steel, much nicer finish and there's a gasket to seal it tightly. And there's extra padding to cushion your loved one for eternity. It's about nine hundred dollars or so more."

So for another thousand bucks we keep out the bugs and Florida's torrential rains. This douche is upselling my parents right now. And they're falling for it because, really, what else are they going to do for their dead twenty-two-year-old daughter? I feel the dry heaves inching their way into my throat but I swallow hard. If Jen were here, she'd want me to keep it together. Any time I was freaking out about something she would say, *You got this, little sister.* I swear I can hear her voice.

I adjust my invisible armor.

"What about this one?" I point to a metal casket that has a slight sheen of pinkish purple to it, with a plum-colored shiny fabric inside and a nice fluffy pillow.

"That's one of our premium caskets. It comes with a triple-reinforced concrete exterior vault that houses the casket. The lid is finished with ninety-nine pounds of non-rusting bronze. It's specially designed to prevent water seepage."

He's a pro, like a used-car salesman. He always has a comeback. An answer for any doubt. Seal the deal.

My parents look like deer caught in headlights. It's all so much.

"Purple is her favorite color," I remind my parents. "The plum pillow … she loved all her pillows." Seeing the resolve on my face, they agree.

"Let's do this one." Hearing my father's voice I realize he can't withstand much more of this absurdity either. Right now I'm caught up in a moment of love for my parents. It might be worse to lose a daughter than a sister.

Might.

We follow Mr. Barnes back to his office like lemmings marching off a cliff. Mom leans in to Dad. "How much did he say that was? I stopped listening."

"It doesn't matter. It's the last thing we are ever going to give our child."

I have to turn away.

Dad sits himself down in front of the funeral director's imposing desk while Mr. Barnes ushers my mom and me over to several binders filled with customizable remembrance cards and psalms.

"These will be handed out to each of your guests upon arrival at the church," he announces, like we're prepping for a party.

Choosing just the perfect card with just the right message becomes my mission, like the casket. It's imperative we get it correct. Words mean everything to Jen. *Meant.* There's no margin for error. But the binders are full of crap.

"Look at these, they're just terrible," I point out. "Jesus. Mom," I say, grabbing her hand. "This one is velvet, like, feel it. Gross, who would use this?" Not gonna lie, this one makes me chuckle. Even Jen would laugh. Not my Mom, though.

"It's just a card, Kai." My mom is near the end of her rope. But I can't give up. I won't.

"It's more than that to me. Words, cards. They were our thing." I'm begging.

I keep flipping the pages. "Birds. Seashells. Tacky. No thank you. "Why is everything a religious reference?" I ask. I read aloud to drive my point home. "'The Lord giveth and the Lord taketh away ...' Well, no shit, but we aren't using this one."

"Kai, your mouth," Mom scolds.

"The twenty-third psalm. 'The Lord blah blah.' Seriously?"

Mom interrupts me. "I like that one."

"No. It's better than the others but I think they're all so dramatic, too much. You know?"

"I just want this to be over." My mom's voice is frozen.

My head is pounding like there's a jackhammer trapped in my skull. I need an aspirin, and I think there's one in my bag. A miracle. And then another: when I reach into the bag, my hand finds a card. From Jen. I yank it out and almost smile. "Mom?"

I reveal a postcard Jen sent me from Dublin, with an Irish blessing on the front. I've kept it in my purse since the day it came in the mail.

May the road rise up to meet you.
May the wind be always at your back.
May the sun shine warm upon your face,
And the rains fall soft upon your fields.
And until we meet again,
May God hold you in the palm of his hand.

Mom sniffs. I reach for her. "This is it. Jen would like this one. Jen loved Ireland. When she was in Dublin, she was in a pub and The

Script played an impromptu set. Like there were maybe twenty-five people there. She said being there felt how magic might feel."

It was a bucket-list moment for her to see them and U2 in Ireland. She never thought it would happen. They're on my list, too.

Mom nods. "Maybe use purple ink to highlight it?"

"Genius, Mom. Instead of her photo on the front — she would hate all that attention — let's use a picture of the beach. She loved the water," I suggest.

"How about the one hanging in her bedroom? The picture she took of the black sand in Maui from our vacation."

Finally we're on the same page. The deep breath I inhale is for both of us.

Mr. Barnes discusses the final arrangements as Dad autographs the never-ending paperwork for Jen's new home.

"The casket will be closed for the service as you requested. But you will have an opportunity to say goodbye privately beforehand. Would you like the casket open or closed for that?"

Dad turns to us.

"Closed," Mom jumps in.

"I have to see her to say goodbye," I plead.

He and my mom start the eyeball speak. Their own private nonverbal language.

"Please." I sniffle.

My mom takes my hand and nods at my father.

"Open," Dad says, gulping down his misery.

* * *

All the hours, all the days blend together. Baskets, flowers, food, they all keep coming. An endless swarm of heartache. Dad sips Johnnie Blue while Mom parks herself at the table reading the cards from each and every arrangement, crying some more. "'We're so sorry for your loss. The Boones,'" Mom reads, and closes the card before adding, "I sold them their condo."

"'May God be with you during this trying time. We are here for you. The Samuels.'" Mom reads my mind: "One of your father's clients."

"This one's for you, Kai." She slides the card across the table to me.

"'We're so sorry about your sister. Hang in there. Love, the yearbook staff.'" I well up.

"What are we supposed to do with all of this?" I ask.

Mom stares blankly at me before she pushes aside the mound of condolence cards, stands quickly with a purpose. She starts setting up what looks like command central. She flings open her laptop, props her iPad upright in its bright blue neoprene case and takes out a legal-size notepad that I see is filled with notes: *DVD of pictures on loop: yes. Taco bar?: yes. Carnitas or chicken: maybe both?* Good God, she even has a Bluetooth headset on like she's an air-traffic controller.

"When can we go to Jen's apartment? We need her outfit. No black."

"Later tonight or tomorrow. I've got a conference call with the caterers in a few minutes." She sorts through her endless lists of lists.

"Caterers?"

"After the service we're having a celebration of Jen's life."

"Can't it just be us? Why does it have to be a thing?"

"Kai, don't be ridiculous. Between your father's firm and my business, not to mention all of Jen's friends, we'll have at least a hundred and fifty guests."

"It's not a party," I point out.

The shrill of the landline muffles my request. Yes, we actually have one, along with three cordless phones Dad bought at Best Buy when we moved in. He does random things like that all the time. Between us we have at least six phones in this house. Like with his mail quirk, Dad's convinced someone may need to reach us and every cell tower in South Florida will be down at that very important moment. Hence the landline.

She trades her headset for a handheld phone.

My dad looks over, quiets his voice. "She has to do this, Kai. She doesn't know what else to do."

"I don't think tacos with a bunch of strangers is going to help."

I don't know whether to laugh or cry. She's going to produce a full-on event. A three-ring circus of mourners shoveling food down their throats and sucking down booze while my sister is twenty minutes away.

Alone.

Six feet underground.

Chapter 5

Still no answers. Not even when my mother and I scoured Jen's apartment at my insistence. Instead, what I found were all of her cookbooks neatly stacked on the granite counter just like the T-shirts in her closet, only not color coordinated. When my eyes landed on the drain board next to the sink, I spotted the birthday gift I gave my sister two years ago. Jen drank her coffee every day from that mug. Part of her morning ritual. I held it close to my heart like that might help; it didn't but I took the cup home anyway. At least the inscription gave me a sliver of joy: MY SISTER HAS AN AWESOME SISTER ... TRUE STORY.

I started collecting souvenirs, not finding clues or answers.

Not even when we painstakingly selected the outfit she would be buried in. In fact, that whole scenario was a gargantuan clusterfuck. The selection of clothing items we stockpiled from her apartment strewn across the sofa in our family room for our perusal. Short dresses, long dresses, jeans, dressy pants, skirts, a blazer, an olive-green military-style jacket, high heels in various heights, Chucks, you name it. The ritual of death I could really do without. Every detail required undivided attention and led to an argument. Mom and I patrolled the couch testing different outfits while my dad nursed his scotch and looked on in silence, hoping to avoid getting caught in the cross fire of our heated funeral-wear exchanges.

"The dress she wore for her graduation party, she looked so beautiful," Mom suggests, pointing to a teal satiny strapless dress.

"Too dressy," I fire back.

"What about the paisley shift dress? She loved that," Mom tosses out, trying.

"Jen was more classic casual. I know she loved her dresses, but jeans and anything from her Madewell collection is what we should go with. And her Chucks, for sure. All of her favorites."

"I'm not burying my child in jeans," Mom says, all offended. She's getting hot-under-the-collar agitated and so am I. Dad is taking a dive headfirst into his bottle of Johnnie Walker, while Mom and I battle over the finalists for the What's Jen Going to Be Buried In? contest.

"It's not about you," I hit back.

"She isn't wearing jeans!" Mom yells.

"Why the hell not?"

One battle after another until my father makes the humongous mistake of weighing in himself.

"It doesn't matter, she's dead."

Let's just say that goes over as one would expect. I completely lose my shit. I mean the kind of losing it where a table gets turned over and unspeakable words are spoken to my parents. The melee sends me storming upstairs punctuating every step with a stomp that echoes all the way up to the landing and retreating into the comfort of a bottle of vodka I swiped and a giant bowl of Blue Dream in my pot pipe.

* * *

My throat is bone-dry. I guzzle a long drink from the water fountain outside the passageway of St. Patrick's. A distorted face looks back at me as I screw up my nose, making a face at myself in the reflection of the aluminum bowl. My mouth is filled with the metallic tang of water fountain H_2O.

I pause outside the chapel where my sister lies in a metal coffin, the best that money can buy. I've stalled as much as humanly possible. It was my idea to see her one last time.

I open my clutch and snap my emergency Xanax in half. I put it under my tongue and steel myself to say a final farewell to my only sibling.

My trembling hand reaches for the maroon velvet curtain behind the pulpit, pulling it open to let myself in. It's all very regal, other than the coffin holding court center stage. I catch a glimpse of my sister's hair and my anxiety level skyrockets through the roof. My parents are in the pew directly in front of the coffin.

Selecting an outfit for each of us wasn't any easier than selecting one for her; there's no real protocol for death clothing other than black and she was pretty clear about that. We each made shades of purple part of our wardrobe along with requisite sunglasses. I carefully chose a dark grape pencil skirt and light pink sleeveless top. Mom went a bit more classic and refined in an eggplant dress with Tory Burch sandals. Dad went with a dark violet-print tie he picked up yesterday at Hugo Boss to complement his navy suit. How bizarre is that? Shopping for a funeral tie like he doesn't have dozens hanging on the tie rack in his closet.

Not a shred of black in sight unless you count my heart, but no one can really see that. "She looks beautiful," Mom says to Dad. It echoes in here. He hands her a tissue. Dad sees me approaching the dais.

"Kai, do you want me to go up there with you?"

"No, I want to be alone with her and recite it."

It's not every day you see a loved one lying peacefully in a coffin. Her makeup and hair are spot-on. The outfit is perfection. Her shiny chestnut hair, not a strand out of place, touching the collar of her boyfriend blazer ever so slightly. Gone is the blue tint to her skin, replaced with a natural tan. Not like a spray-on orange tan, but a light makeup applied to her face, the kind that could pass for the color in your cheeks after a day at the beach. Nothing phony about it. Mr. Barnes and his prep team nailed their hideous task.

I remind myself that this is what she wanted. She wanted to die. It's a mantra in my head. *Her choice. Her choice. Her choice.* I notice Mom's diamond necklace around her neck, lying perfectly against Jen's neck. My sister loved that thing. She used to say, *I get that when you die,* teasing our mom. It's a simple diamond heart on a silver chain. Simple and beautiful like Jen. I bend so close to her.

"I don't think I can do this, Jen Jen," I whisper. "Me without you just doesn't fit."

The ugly cry takes over. My parents stand back and allow my grief to pour down my face as I continue my conversation with my sister.

"Remember the article I sent you on Charlotte Brontë? The one I wrote for the *Wildcat Review*? I hope you understood that the quote I highlighted in the article was for you."

I reach inside my bag, taking out the written quote. I fold the note in half and tuck it under the left side of her blazer so it will be close to her heart forever. I lean in next to her and recite it.

"You know full well as I do the value of sisters' affection: There is nothing like it in this world."

"Will there ever be anything like that again for me?" I ask her.

The answer to that is the same as before: a resounding *no effing way.*

* * *

Though it's eighty-plus degrees, my body is shivering. I rub my hand over my bare arm, willing it to stop shaking. Flanked by my mom and dad graveside, I pretty much switch to autopilot. My shades have stayed on for the entire church service and I've gone through every Kleenex I could get my clammy hands on.

A few days ago my parents painstakingly toured the grounds of Lauderdale Memorial Park, the oldest, most prestigious cemetery in Fort Lauderdale, and decided on the prime real estate near a two-hundred-year-old oak tree with a nearby waterfall. Jen loved the sound of rushing water, any kind of water really. They were honoring her desire to be at peace. We all were, no matter how much it was destroying each one of us day by day.

As we're staring at the closed casket housing my sister, with grave straps dangling it over a person-size hole in the ground, it's only fitting that an afternoon rain shower falls on us. Even the sky weeps for our loss. TJ hands me an umbrella but I push it away.

"I want to feel every miserable moment of this," I say to him. We both know I really don't want to feel anything. That would spare me this suffering.

Father Michael, dressed in a funeral robe, all black except for a royal blue sash, concludes the service with the Lord's Prayer: "... forgive us our trespasses as we forgive those who trespass against us ..."

He didn't comply with the no-black rule, but arguing with a priest couldn't possibly end well. The wind muffles the rest of the prayer. I despise all the mourners for no other reason than that they are here.

Father Michael grabs a shovel and tosses some dirt on my sister, then passes it to my parents, who mindlessly do the same. When Dad puts the shovel in my hand, I throw it to the rain-soaked ground.

"I'm not throwing dirt on her." Emily grabs my hand and we retreat before I explode. TJ backs away with us.

"I'm so sorry, Kai," Emily mumbles.

"I don't know what else to say," adds TJ.

"There's nothing to say. She's never coming home."

When that hits me like a ton of brick, so do the sobs. My friends do their best to hold me up, one on each side of me, propping me upright. My mom places her arm around my waist, leading me to the limousine.

"Kai, we have to go."

I comply like my five-year-old self would have, never looking back, but I hear them start to lower her into the cold, hard ground alone.

I will never forget the whirring of the grinding gears.

Ever.

* * *

Christ, it's party time at the Sheehans'. Fucking unbelievable. Dear God, there's a margarita machine on the patio. My house is overflowing with people. All our neighbors. Families. Jen's college friends. A slew of people I've never laid eyes on, they didn't even know my sister. Who are they? It's a three-ring circus.

Emily takes my hand.

"If one more person says, 'I'm so sorry for your loss,' I will rip my hair out strand by strand. Or if they mention what a wonderful girl Jen was, I will go postal," I say.

Emily holds me.

"I swear to Christ, every single time anyone mentions her name, she dies one more time. Over and over and over."

"Let's go outside. TJ already hijacked a pitcher of margaritas. One of the hot catering waiters hooked him up."

That almost makes me laugh.

"I can't. I have to be the hostess with the mostest. You see my parents." We watch my mom and dad working the crowd like politicians. They're on autopilot, too.

"I have to talk to Jen's friends first."

She presses her shoulder to mine. Something we've been doing since we met. No words necessary.

I spot my sister's squad and start to make a beeline toward them, dodging some neighbors who moved away years ago. Is there anyone who isn't here? Tracy, my sister's college roommate, is the first to envelop me, her firm grip grounding me. Marlene and Bethany follow suit, all swallowed up in their own grief. They were the Four Musketeers. Surely one of them can help me put the pieces together.

Bethany breaks the circle of Jen love. "Kai, this must be so surreal." Her voice drifts as her eyes drip like a leaky faucet.

I charge ahead. "Did any of you suspect this could happen? I can't figure out what was so terrible in her life that she would do this."

"I mean, she was bummed that a guy she was hooking up with from work only thought of her as a friend but … no big deal. Right?" Tracy offers up. I don't know if it's a big deal or not since I didn't even know there was a guy. Another secret? Now, I'm really mad. She turned my life upside down and left me with nothing but secrets and lies.

"Is he even here?" Not that it matters, but if he is, I'm going to kill him.

Tracy and Marlene both shake their heads, draining their wineglasses.

"I wish we could help you, Kai. The truth is we've all been running over every text, every call, and if there was any sign, we missed it," Bethany says, her voice consumed with a grief and guilt I know well.

Misery loves company.

"Can I do anything, Kai?" Tracy asks.

"I wish you could. All my parents keep talking about is things getting back to normal. Jen killing herself is anything but normal."

"They aren't thinking clearly. You have to remember that they don't have a normal anymore either," she rationalizes.

With that thought stuck in my head, I wander through the backyard to meet Emily and TJ. My phone vibrates. When I slide it out of my pocket, I see a text from Marlene. It's a picture of me with the Four Musketeers from Jen's freshman year, with a message: *Love this pic.*

That margarita machine is calling my name. I start to pull the metal handle back with my free hand but nothing comes out.

"Let me give you a hand," a voice says from behind me.

I twist back to see a guy who looks kind of familiar but I can't place him. He's flashing me a grin. He reaches around me, brushing my shoulder, to move the handle back and forth a few times. Then a miracle happens. The frozen drink flows into my cup like a soft-serve ice-cream cone.

"Thanks," I say. I start to leave but he stops me, taking my elbow in his hand.

"Jake. Your sister used to babysit me. We met ages ago. I had braces back then?" He tries to jog my memory.

"Sorry, I don't remember."

"Ouch. I had such a crush on you," he says. Pretty sure I'm glowing red. "You're just as cute as you were when you were eight. We should hang out sometime."

I take a long sip before I attempt to sidestep this awkward. "Jake, not really a good time." I hold my tongue. *Are you fucking kidding me?*

He sticks his lower lip out and grabs my phone. I watch in utter disbelief as he adds his number to my contacts.

"If you change your mind," he says before he hands it back.

That happens.

I silently thank my mom for insisting on the margaritas. The gazebo is in my sights. My parents argued about whether we really needed such a thing. Dad thought the saltwater pool and redwood deck were plenty for the backyard. Mom won the battle and added a brick fireplace for good measure even though it's only cold enough one or two days a year to put it to good use.

"Finally," TJ says. "We were worried about you."

I throw myself on the chaise next to him. "This day."

He tops off my drink.

"I have to get out of here."

TJ puts his arm around my shoulder. "Can you escape tonight? Houser's dock party is gonna be epic. They got a band and a keg."

All I can do is sigh, knowing there's no way my parents would let me go even if I wanted to. If I'm being honest, I do kinda want to go. You know, do something a regular teenager would be doing on a Saturday night. Instead, I'm trapped in hell. Thanks, Jen. Jesus, now I'm pissed at my dead sister.

* * *

The last of the waiters are hauling dishes out to the catering van. I continue to stare from my bedroom window until they drive away. Finally, it's safe to go downstairs. Though the effects of the tequila and general exhaustion are beginning to take their toll, I decide it's a good idea to help clean up. I finish whatever alcohol is inhabiting the highball glasses and wineglasses scattered inside the McMansion. With my parents elsewhere, I systematically make my way around the family room, talking to the dog and myself.

"A quarter of a glass of white wine? Why, thank you, Mrs. Sandler," I mention to Duke, who's following me hoping for a dropped taco or any scrap. He's a chowhound.

I dread the sound of the locking dead bolt on the front door as my father seals us all inside. The finality is undeniable. The population of our family is now officially three.

The silence is deafening.

This is the new normal.

I despise it already.

Chapter 6

I pass on the whole *We're going to pack up your sister's things* activity that my mother is hell-bent on this morning. She woke up armed with a checklist, and cleaning out Jen's apartment is first up. I can't believe my ears when I hear her talking to Dad over coffee.

"The landlord was so kind, so sympathetic when I called him, no problem breaking the lease. He said we could have as much time as we needed to clean out the apartment. May as well get it over with, there's never going to be a good time for this," Mom just blurts.

"You're packing Jen's stuff? Already?" I squeal. "Why can't we just pay the rent and keep it for another month?"

"It's just something we have to take care of," Mom rips back.

"I'm not going," I say.

"You can spend the morning researching colleges other than FSU, you need a fallback school. May as well get a jump on it," Dad suggests.

"I'm taking a gap year," I state flatly. Jen was supposed to tell them, but she was supposed to do a lot of things.

Before I can even lay out my plan, my father flips out.

"No, you're not."

"Yeah, I am." I fight back. "I'm going to Europe just like she did." My voice gets louder with each word and I don't even care.

Mom says, "I think you should wait until you graduate like Jen did."

"What about what I want?"

Mom cuts me off. "Your sister just died, Kai."

I stand up. "Well, I didn't."

My only thought as I rage upstairs, taking two steps at a time, is, *We are so not done with this.* I storm around my room until I hear them leave.

* * *

I'm already overcome with anxiety about going back to the grind of high school. First off, I'll be going from Kai Sheehan, sophomore writer girl, to *The girl whose sister committed suicide.* It was all over social media the day after she died. How could anyone possibly understand? The silver lining is that I'll return to my routine. I'll go to school and every day won't be another thing on the checklist of death. Dad is already back to work, and Mom is slowly easing into things. I'm the only one lagging behind.

I force myself to look at all the assignments I've missed. Two quizzes and an English paper, just last week. I'm even behind on yearbook. Hard to look at all the smiling faces when I've lost mine.

I should study but my mind is on something else. I Google all things Europe in preparation for the gap year that I will be taking come hell or high water. I bookmark Ireland and start a list of my

63

own: Kelsey's Pub in Dublin, fingers crossed for lightning striking twice with The Script. Kissing the Blarney Stone. Cliffs of Moher. Pub crawl. Duh. A quick check of Jen's postcards sends me to Italy next.

I am distracted by a ding on my phone. TJ posted on Instagram. Shit, it's a picture of him and Emily at the beach. Without me. From all the posts, it looks like a barbecue-and-beach-volleyball kind of a day. And here's a picture of Emily and her sister that she posted an hour ago. There's no escape.

I will never have another post with my sibling.

So ... how quickly can I deaden this hurt? Mom couldn't bear to throw away anything with my sister's name on it, not even the vials that held the pills that killed her. I helped myself to a variety of those leftovers when Mom wasn't glued to me. I start with a Vicodin, a couple of Advil and a bowl of weed. Nice combo. Squelch the pain, kill the headache and chill the mind.

Duke's unremitting barking signals the return of my parents. I detach my face from my pillow to steal a quick glance at my phone: 2:45 p.m. Jeez, it took them less than six hours to box up twenty-two years of life. I hear a light rap on my door and I yell, "Come in!" even though I don't mean it.

Mom half smiles when she sees the pillowcase crease on my right cheek.

"I thought you might like to have these," she says, thrusting a box onto my bed. I notice one of Jen's bracelets on Mom's arm, a beaded leather wrap, red and blue teeny beads intricately designed adorning it. Jen picked it up in Morocco at an outdoor market. She notices me notice but neither one of us says anything about it.

I crank back my anger from the morning. She's trying.

I riffle through the box, first unveiling a Kindle, still in the original packaging.

"She loved her books, hated that Kindle we got her. The idea of being able to take so many books with her, we really thought she would love it when she traveled," Mom recalls.

I can't help but crack up. "That was definitely a Christmas-gift fail."

"We boxed up her bookshelves. She had quite the collection, from Seuss to Salinger. I picked out the ones I thought you'd like to keep on your shelf. The rest will be in the garage till we figure everything out."

I mindlessly grab the Kerouac that's sitting on the top.

"This was next to her bed," I say, knowing she probably hasn't forgotten that any more than I have.

"She loved his writing and anything sixties. She was such an old soul. Maybe a little bit of a wanderer like him," Mom says, getting misty.

I start thumbing through it. I stop near a passage that's marked with one of her trademark neon Post-its.

Off to the side in her handwriting, in blue ink: *Amsterdam July with Danielo*.

"She never mentioned anyone named Danielo before, but he must've meant something if she wrote his name in her beloved book. Right, Mom?"

"I have no idea who he was either." Something else she kept from all of us.

I reach in the box and run my fingers down the binding of a book that brings a smile to my lips.

"*Franny and Zooey*, arguably Salinger's best."

"Jen would agree, but I'd have to go with *The Catcher in the Rye*," Mom mutters as she absentmindedly folds the heap of laundry at the end of my bed. One more thing I haven't got around to doing. I open Jen's journal of quotes and sayings and see an orange Post-it fixed to a Walt Whitman quote.

"I exist as I am — that is enough."

I read it aloud and regret it the second I do, realizing Jen didn't heed Walt's sage advice. Mom and I exchange a knowing look.

"I guess it wasn't enough," I say, overcome with sadness.

Mom can only shake her head, water filling her empty eyes.

Still, I can't help the happiness that sneaks in when I see the book wedged behind her poetry collection. I ease it out of the carton.

"*Big Red Barn* was my favorite because Jen would make all the sounds of the animals as she read aloud to me."

"I remember that," Mom says. "When the house was quiet, we knew exactly where to find you girls. Together, on opposite sides of the couch, each lost in a book, even when you couldn't read. You just liked doing whatever Jen did. You had a very special relationship, Kai. No one can take that away from you."

"I want more time," I choke out.

"We all do."

I chew on that for a moment.

"Mom, why do you think she did it? Why would she want to leave us? What could have been so bad?" I ask.

Mom takes a beat. With a heaviness in her voice she answers, "I wish I knew."

"Have you talked to Dad?"

She sighs. "Honey. It's hard for us to talk about it. He tosses and turns every night. They had an argument about money. She needed help with her credit card payment, and he thought she should be more responsible. It wasn't a huge fight. Your dad didn't think it was a big deal. He blames himself for not seeing what no one did."

"What are we going to do?" I ask, continuing the longest real conversation I've had with my grieving mother about anything that matters.

"Get through it." She stands up, ending the depth of it all.

"We got everything packed up for the movers to take to storage," Mom claims.

There it is. It's back. That uncanny Sheehan ability to turn emotions on and off.

"I'm gonna go get something to drink. Do you want anything?" she asks.

"I'm okay," I reply.

I'm lying.

We're all lying.

Nothing is ever going to be okay again.

Chapter 7

I think I liked it better when we didn't do family dinners every night. Mom's been cooking, a first. She makes a ton of food like she's feeding an army, and Dad pretends to love every bite while he washes it down with a vodka martini, straight up with two olives — never one, never three — and a twist. Tonight is our first Sunday back at the dining room table. That hits me in the gut while I'm setting the table. The torment is magnified when I stare across the table at the empty chair.

"Smells great," I lie to my mom, watching her slice and dice cabbage and potatoes.

"Thanks, sweetie. Dad will be home in about an hour. He went to run an errand with Mr. Lancaster."

"I'm gonna take the dog for a walk before dinner."

As I put Duke's leash on, he rubs up against me and almost purrs. "Let's go, buddy." His wagging tail slaps against my legs but I don't mind, it reminds me I'm still alive.

Alive means it's okay to go to the Calvin Harris show next week, or is it? Jen would know the answer but I can't really ask her. She got tickets for us a few months ago. She was taking me and TJ. I took the tickets off her dresser when Mom and I went to her house to pick up the outfit she would be buried in.

"What do you think, Duke? Should I go? It *is* Calvin Harris. Is that shitty or okay?" He keeps walking and wagging.

"Not helping," I say.

He cranes his neck back, like he's smiling at me. I take that as a yes.

A few weeks ago, I could just pick up the phone and call my sister to get her opinion on anything. Now I'm relying on her dog.

The warm tropical breeze is a welcome relief. The humidity is low and there's zero chance of rain in the forecast, according to my weather app. Passing by the matching houses in our cookie-cutter community, I pray no one is outside watering their expansive lawn or washing their car. Last night, half the neighborhood was outdoors for our walk and half of those people had to comment on the recent death of my sister. Weren't their condolences at the funeral enough? Every time they ask how we're all getting along, I want to scream, *How the fuck do you think we are?* But I refrain. My answer is always the same: *We are all okay.*

Sniffing every blade of grass and tree in sight, Duke finally selects the Hastingses' sweeping front lawn to do his business. I'm half tempted to leave it there knowing I'd get a bye because of my circumstance, but I see Old Lady Hastings peering out the window over her glasses, dressed in her flowered housecoat, so I blue-bag it and we head home. About a block or so from the house, Duke suddenly yanks on his leash — and on me — nearly sending me sprawling in the Lancasters' driveway. Barking relentlessly, he jerks on the leash like he's been possessed by the devil.

"What's the matter, buddy?" I almost expect him to answer. I make a feeble attempt at calming him down, cupping his head and scratching his back, but he is a dog on a mission.

"Crazy dog." But he isn't letting up one little bit. I look down the street to see what set him off.

Then I see it. Suddenly it's hard to swallow; my eyes fill with familiar stinging. Smack in the middle of our driveway is Jen's black Toyota 4Runner.

My dad's errand.

As we get closer, Duke gets more and more excited, his tail whipping around a mile a minute, his bark filled with hope. He doesn't understand what I know all too well. His favorite human in the world did not come home with the car.

Duke loves riding in the backseat to the beach, his oversize golden head hanging out the window, catching wind all the way down the A1A, making a mess on the windows with his drool and hot breath. I grab the door handle hoping my dad forgot to lock it. He's been off his game since my sister died. The click of the lever and Duke's joy confirm my suspicions. Even my dad can't focus. I swing the back door open. "Okay, boy."

He leaps in the back, sniffs around and lies down on top of one of the many stray sweatshirts that live in her truck. I join him, wadding one up to rest next to him. I stroke his ears and face as I explain the inexplicable.

"Sorry, buddy, she's gone. Not like when she went to Europe. She isn't coming back to us. Ever. But hey, you have me."

If my tears on his back bother him, he doesn't let on. He noses my hand. I cuddle closer, almost spooning him.

It's where Mom finds us an hour later. When she goes to pick up the mail.

Chapter 8

Dread greets me when TJ and I get to school. My first day back. The moment we get into the quad, all eyes are on me. Or at least I think they are.

TJ takes my hand. "You'll be okay. I'm right here with you."

I kiss his cheek.

A group of football players walk by. "Hey, Kai. Sorry about your sister." They nod and keep walking.

"They've barely said a word to me in the last year. God," I groan.

We run into Bridget and Kate from yearbook. They stop to welcome me back. "Kai, we're here if you need anything." All four of us get weepy eyed. I tug on TJ's hand to keep us moving. I can't afford the meltdown that's brewing. No one wants to see me break, especially me.

The whispering is even more unbearable than the silent staring. I guess no one really knows what to do.

The guidance counselor meets us in the office.

"Kai, you know we were all very sorry to hear about your sister."

"It's okay," I say like I mean it.

TJ tightens his grip on my hand.

"I've talked to your teachers, they're going to give you makeup tests to take at home when you're ready."

Now I'm a special case at school, too?

"It's okay, Mr. Condon, if everyone else took them here, I'll do the same."

His eyes pity me. I've seen that glazed-over, poor-kid look about a hundred times. At least.

"Kai, no one expects you to catch up your first week back."

"Really, I'm good."

TJ side-eyes me. I know he's thinking, *Take this deal, it's sweet.* He doesn't get it. No one does. I just want it to be the way it was before.

"If you need to leave early or anything, it's okay."

Nothing is going to be okay, Mr. Condon.

The rest of the day is pretty much the same. Even my teachers are walking on eggshells. No one calls on me. No one asks for my homework.

Two more classes, then I'm home free. TJ and I are going to McDonald's. Ah, normal.

I ease into a desk halfway up the second aisle, the only empty one other than the three in the front row.

"Dude, her sister offed herself. Who does that?" John Lozano not-so whispers to Janie Dankins, one of the girls I played Pop Warner softball with when I was seven. High school put some distance between us. Her clique deems anyone who writes for the newspaper too geeky for them. She sucked at softball anyway.

"Her sister was weird," Janie adds.

My head snaps back and I turn into someone I don't know. My eyes rip her insides out.

"Why don't you shut the fuck up about something you know nothing about?"

Stuttering, she attempts to backtrack. "I — I didn't mean anything ... I mean, it's just really horrible."

"Really? If you didn't mean anything, why did you open your mouth?" I snarl at her. I'm pretty sure I'm showing teeth. I notice a few of my classmates cower a bit. AP English just got ugly.

"It's just —"

I throw my fist in her direction, practically coming out of my seat, pulling back just inches before actually punching her in the face, which she richly deserves. But it's against school policy. So I don't.

She shrieks just enough to get any attention that wasn't already focused on our altercation. That idiot John Lozano is doing his best imitation of a statue ever. Motionless and ever so quiet.

"Look, you narcissistic bitch, if you say one more word about my sister, this fist will rearrange that phony face of yours and I'll gladly get expelled for doing it."

I slam my book closed, squeeze out of my desk and get the hell out of there as fast as my legs can move.

A few snickers along with a few flat-out gasps accompany my rapid departure before the bell. I rush to the first girls' bathroom I can duck into. Kicking open the door of the last stall, I crawl up onto the toilet, tucking one foot under the other, turn the stainless steel lock on the door to the right and bawl for the entire period.

The shrill sound of the bell jars me. I try to collect myself before anyone comes in between classes but I'm not quick enough. The door swooshes open followed by the sound of footsteps. I recognize Janie's snotty voice but not the other girl's. Not that it matters.

"Did you see the way she flipped out right in the middle of class? She's straight-up crazy," says Janie.

"Jesus. Cut her some slack, her sister just died," the other voice argues.

"Killed herself. People who *just die* don't want to. She did."

I hate to give the bitch any credit but she's right on the money. Still, it hurts. A lot. I will the tears to stop running down my face as I slowly open the stall. When they see me in the mirror, they both turn varying shades of red and start fumbling with the faucets. I stride past them with my head held high, directly out the swinging door.

I think I'll take Mr. Condon up on his offer. I make my way down the hallowed halls of Parkland High. *Just keep putting one sandal in front of the other*, I tell myself. *Do not look up.* For when I do glance in any direction, all I see looking back at me is judgment. Emily races down the hall, moving pretty fast for a girl in such a short skirt and heels.

"You okay?"

"Yeah," I say. I'm starting to get good at this. *Yeah, folks, I'm fine. Why wouldn't I be?*

"Just getting used to being back."

She bear-hugs me.

"I have to get to class," I say, eyeballing the flickering red EXIT sign at the far end of the History hallway, estimating the number of times I will need to put one foot in front of the other before I press that door's metal bar and free myself from this hell.

"See you later?" Em asks.

"Yeah, sure." Getting really good. I wave, and as soon as she's out of my sight line, I stride straight out of school. I keep going until I can no longer see the building or any of those faces riddled with pity.

When I make my way a few blocks down the main road to the local park, it's nearly desolate, only a few people congregating at this early hour. Stay-at-home moms swinging their children on a red swing set close to the winding slide, never imagining that one day one of them might take their own life. Just innocently enjoying the glorious Florida sunshine. I sneak behind the bathrooms with my backpack and remove the last of the airplane bottles of Smirnoff that TJ smuggled over to me. The clear liquid tingles as it goes down but it's a welcome breather. I use it to wash down a Xanax because I need to quiet my brain. Then I wrap the empty bottle in a piece of notebook paper, toss it in the chipped green trash can and scan the park for a place to clear my head.

The sound of a text jars me.

I just heard. She's an asshole. Ignore her. See you after school. Xo Em

Earbuds jammed in my ears, I make myself at home under a palm tree. The soothing sound of Bon Iver, one of Jen's favorites, is precisely what I need.

Drifting off, I'm seven years old on a swing in my backyard yelling at the top of my lungs, "Higher, higher!" My dad built us one of those monster cedar playsets with a slide, a deck with a ladder and a swing. I was the envy of everyone in the neighborhood. As my size-six, midnight-blue Chuck Taylors point straight up in the air, I'm flying. Pure, unadulterated joy. The kind of bliss that only comes when you don't have a care in the world. I look back and see my thirteen-year-old sister smiling that smile, pushing me, cheering me on.

A firm hand shakes my shoulder. The panic jars me back momentarily.

"Are you okay? You were crying so loudly," the tousled-blond-haired mom from the swing set asks.

"Oh, I'm so sorry. Bad dream," I fib, gathering my things.

"Can I call someone? Your mother?" There's such sincerity in her eyes, I think about my mom. I feel blue all over. I hear her cry at night downstairs when she thinks no one hears her. Her own private hell.

"No, thanks. I'm meeting a friend. I must have dozed off. Late night studying."

"Take care," she says as leaves.

No longer able to ignore the dozen frantic calls, I pick up my phone.

"Jesus Christ, where the hell are you? You were supposed to meet me at the Jeep," screeches TJ before I can even say hello. Drama queen.

"I took a walk."

"I heard about Janie."

Of course he did.

"She's a troll, we already knew that. I'm coming to get you. Just tell me where you are."

I start to tell him I'll be fine but I don't. Because I'm not sure that I will be.

"Bixby Park."

We hang up just as a text from my mom appears on my phone.

How's the day, sweetie?

I don't miss a beat.

Fine.

Dinner at 7. Dad's grilling salmon, ok?
Just a regular Monday.
K.

TJ wheels his Jeep into the parking space closest to the stucco-sided bathrooms. He's in such a rush that he takes up two spots. Parking fail. Emily leaps out of the passenger side like a superhero, races over and flings herself onto the grass next to me.

"Oh my God, you're okay," she says hysterically.

"You, too?"

"We were worried about you, Kai. It's your first day back after everything and you get into it with Janie. She's such a loser." I give her a peck on the cheek. She pauses. "You smell like alcohol."

"I just needed to chill, Em." She nods. I know she gets it.

TJ is cradling a cardboard carrier from Ozzy's, one of our favorite food spots. I eyeball the three bowls of frozen yogurt that match his Billabong shirt.

"Peach. Today's special. I even got fresh peaches mixed in."

"Really?"

"It's blazing hot and it seemed refreshing."

"Don't take this the wrong way, but you've never sounded gayer."

He flips me off as he hands us each our bowls. TJ raises his spoon to toast us.

"To a sucky Monday."

The thing about best friends is you don't have to say anything and they know what you need. They also know when to keep quiet. All you need is their presence to drive away all the madness in your life.

"I don't know what I'm gonna do. I miss her so much." My friends reach out for me at the same time and twenty fingers pull me into the safety zone.

Just not the fingers I miss the most.

Chapter 9

Staring into my bathroom mirror, caking concealer over the dark circles under my eyes, I still can't believe I got talked into going to this stupid dance. If you look up *last thing Kai Sheehan wants to do ever*, it would scream in bright white blinking lights, GO TO THIS HIGH SCHOOL PROM.

I hear my bedroom door open and duck out to find Emily in a form-fitting orange tank dress looking all perky and stunning. Two things I am not.

"You know I hate everything about going to this dance, right?" I say emphatically, adjusting my sleeveless polka-dot dress, then slipping into my soft-pink wedge sandals. I'm fairly certain that my best friends and my parents have been conspiring to get me to the prom since Jen died. Frankly, they wore me down until I acquiesced.

"I know this is messed up and ridiculously hard, but you know how much fun we had at the last dance you didn't want to go to."

She makes a good point. We snuck a six-pack in for that one.

"Come on, Kai. We can just let loose," Emily suggests. "And we have to go for yearbook, so …"

Damn, she's right. I pop a Xanax into my mouth and let it dissolve under my tongue. I don't even mind the chalky aftertaste. It takes effect much quicker this way. Emily just watches, brow slightly raised, lips zipped.

"Letting loose sounds fine. Fun? I don't know how to do that anymore."

She grabs my hand. "I'm really worried about you, Kai. You seem so … I don't know … unengaged. You've missed the last two yearbook meetings, you barely respond to our group texts, you didn't even mention the new music from The 1975."

"Em, please, don't psychobabble me. You sound like my mom."

TJ walks in, saving Emily from any further wrath. He opens his arms wide to show off his powder-blue tuxedo.

"Rad, right?"

"Hot as ever," Emily compliments him.

"This bitch is going to glow in the dark on the dance floor underneath the lights. I can't wait." He's bubbling over like this is some epic event.

Clearly I'm the only one not happy about this. *Make lemonade from the lemons.* A Jen favorite. I dig into my overflowing laundry basket and hoist a bottle of Tito's Handmade Vodka in the air like the trophy it is. "Surprise!"

TJ slow-claps me. "Nicely done. But how did you get that?"

"Got it out of one of the condolence baskets. Thank you, Jen."

Emily cringes.

Both my parents have been off their game and tiptoeing around me. I suspect I've got some leeway here and I plan to take every inch of it. I hear the whispers late at night when they think I'm sleeping. Oddly, they never talked this much when Jen was alive, both too busy with their careers to remember we were a family. Truth: it didn't really bother me because I had Jen. Now they're both lost in their worlds like I am in mine.

Once Jen left for college, my parents both hit their peak at work, leaving very little family time other than Sunday dinners, the once-a-semester sojourn to visit Jen and our yearly family vacation. The one where the annual Christmas-card pictures were taken. Dad worked late every night, then ate his dinner in the man cave with ESPN on a loop. Mom threw herself into real estate, which started out as a hobby, but anyone who knows my mom knows that she has to be the best. And damn, she's good. She could sell a cape to Superman.

"Let's get going," TJ says.

"Do we have to?" I try to switch it up.

"Five minutes, ten max," Emily promises.

Like a dog with a bone.

I relent. "Okay, okay. We can do a drive-by. I need to do that anyway, just to take some pictures in the parking lot. You know, for my mom. We'll go inside for a few minutes to snap a few more for posting to prove we went, then we are outta there. Mom's been lurking on Twitter since Jen died. My Instagram is an alert on her phone."

The three of us stage a mini–photo shoot beginning in the middle of the parking lot at our high school.

"I want to be in the middle." TJ jumps up and down like a maniac, planting his powder-blue torso between us.

"Hey, can you take a picture of us?" Emily stops some random passerby in the junior lot as she thrusts her phone at him, leaving him no option.

We strike a few poses, varying our positions, Em and I perfectly positioning our hands on our hips to avoid any unflattering side views. Just the right jutting of the hip and perfect centering of our hands.

"See if you like these or need me to take more?" he says, showing Emily the pictures on her phone.

We all lean in to scrutinize them.

"Post-worthy," I say as I download a picture for my mom to find. BEST NIGHT EVER AT THE DANCE WITH EM AND TJ.

"Thanks, man," TJ says as the photo guy goes back to his group of friends.

"He was cute," I comment.

"The dark suit was standard but the way he filled it was not," TJ notes, watching him strut away.

"Really? He's so not your type," I crack.

"Maybe I'm stepping out of my comfort zone."

"Um, okay," I say.

"The necklace is dope," TJ says, noticing the clear quartz crystal with black flecks of tourmaline hanging from a cord of black leather.

"Jen got it for me when she was in Brazil. It's supposed to keep you safe."

"I remember." TJ strokes the nape of my neck. His touch soothes me for a moment.

After a shot or three of vodka, we weave through the parking lot of stoners and cheerleaders piling out of a limo and slip unnoticed through the double steel doors of the school auditorium.

"Looks like Katie Hanson and the decorating team worked overtime transforming the drab auditorium into a Starry Nights extravaganza," observes TJ. He sees me give him the look. "I know I sound a little queeny, but come on, look around." I have to admit he's one-hundred-percent correct. I bow down to him.

"I love the glow-in-the-dark stars." They cover the ceiling, which is veiled with black lights that turn the walls into a purple haze. "I wouldn't mind those in my room," I add. Another something I could get lost in.

"We can totally do that," Emily offers.

Luminescent white twinkle lights drape gently over the palm trees they've rented from the local nursery. It's impressive, and under different circumstances I might even enjoy myself.

But being here ... with all the laughter ... I want the old me back. I want to join in but all this does is remind me of Jen. She took me shopping for a new dress before my first dance in middle school. Insisted I go when I didn't want to. She promised I'd have a good time if I just gave it a chance. I know she'd say the same tonight. But I just can't. Not without her. It's not right.

TJ and I pose under the glittery STARRY NIGHTS sign near the photo booth. Emily hands me back my phone.

"I'm saving that to strategically post later."

"You don't actually think your mom is gonna buy this, do you? It's a little over the top even for us," TJ asks, filled with doubt.

My sense of calm from the vodka dissipates and anxious terror takes over once I zero in on the maroon writing on the band's drum set: STEELHEART.

I feel the color drain from my face and invisible fingers grab hold of my heart, then wrench it. Hard. That familiar feeling of heartbreak creeps back in. Suddenly sophomore year is like yesterday.

Though he was a supreme douchebag, I have to give Chris Santini props: At least he was discreet. He never shared our story with his bros.

His only plus.

That, and he played the drums. For Steelheart.

TJ scoops his powder-blue arm around my waist. "Time to go." We walk with purpose toward the back door, flagging down Emily. "Emily knows where the car is, she can meet us."

"It's just —" I start to explain.

He stops and turns me, squaring me up directly in front of him. "I know, Kai. You don't want to be here, you don't want to see Chris and you're drowning in unimaginable grief. We're here to protect you. Let us do our job."

I take his face in my hands. "I don't know what I'd do without you."

"That is one thing you'll never have to worry about," he replies with such conviction that I have to believe it is true.

By the time Emily joins our mini-party next to the Jeep, I've killed half a joint and a few swigs of lukewarm Budweiser.

"Let's go to the beach, your sister loved it there. We can have our own party," she says.

TJ kisses my forehead.

"I love you guys." I slur just a bit.

I'm pretty sure I flash anyone in the nearby vicinity. There is no ladylike way to climb into a Jeep with a dress this short. TJ eases into the driver's seat, cranks up the engine and puts the car in reverse. It's always a victory when the ignition turns over. Gertie can be a little testy like the rest of us.

We peel out of the school parking lot, leaving the pavement and this glimmering soiree in the dust.

The moment I hear the waves roll in, crashing on the sand, I know it was right of Emily to insist we come here. TJ opens a diet orange soda, pours out half of it, then replaces it with vodka. We pass it around quietly, listening to the lulling sound of the water rushing back and forth on the mostly white sand across from the Holiday Inn on A1A.

A blustery wind coming off the open sea kicks up, causing our hair to whip all over our faces and the sand to exfoliate our cheeks. I throw myself back on the fuzzy beach blanket and count the stars and wonder what else is up there, if anything.

"Do you believe there's a heaven?" I ask my two closest friends.

"I'm not sure. Conceptually, it's a hard sell. Emotionally, if you don't think so, what do you have to hang on to?" Emily reasons.

"Buddhists believe rebirth after death can take place in any number of existences. Heaven is a temporary place you gain access to according to the manner you lived your life in before death," TJ pontificates.

"Seriously?" I ask. My voice is dripping with sarcasm.

"We're studying it in Religion. It makes some sense." He takes off his jacket and bow tie and unbuttons the top few buttons of his shirt.

"If you believe in some kind of heaven, do you have to believe in God?" I can't let this go.

"I don't know if you have to, but I definitely believe in God. Don't you?" Emily asks.

"No. If there was a God, he never would have let my sister take her own life." I unscrew the cap on the vodka bottle and wash down that acrimonious dose of reality.

"I'm so ragey all the time. It's like I forgot happy," I admit.

TJ takes my hand. "You'll find it again. Time." The ocean looks so peaceful, lit by a multitude of tiny lights in the universe over our beach. I want to reach up and grab one but I know I can't. What I can do is grab one of the millions of twinkling lights swooping in and out with each wave. Touch the stars in the water with my very own hands.

I leap up, peeling off my dress, and race to the freedom of the vast, inviting ocean.

"What the hell are you doing?" screeches Emily.

"Going swimming!" I hit the water's edge, and the wet sand squishes between my toes, then the cool water washes over my feet, working its way up my legs. God, it's like stepping into a constellation. I keep going, diving under, swimming straight out into nothingness.

"Kai!" TJ's voice gets more and more faint. My arms grow weary after a few minutes and my legs start to weigh me down. The warm, salty water feels so soothing on my skin. I close my eyes, then slip under the surface and let myself drift with the current. It's so freeing. When I pop up from the surf to catch my breath, I squint and see Emily and TJ swimming toward me, screaming something I can't quite make out at first. As they get closer, I realize it's my name.

"Kai!!!"

"I'm okay!" I shout. They don't seem to hear me.

"Kai, don't move. I'll be right there." TJ sounds frantic. His rapid stroke cuts through the water, leaving almost no wake. I dive back under and propel myself toward him. I hear Emily's muffled voice shout my name yet again.

"Kai! Kai, Christ, Kai."

I surface nearby. "What?"

As we all tread water, TJ screams, "Are you fucking crazy? We thought you were going to drown. Drunk fool."

"I'm okay." Other than the invisible ten-pound weights wrapped around all four of my dog-tired limbs.

"I swear to whatever God you don't believe in, if you say that one more time, I will kill you myself," Emily hisses.

"Same," TJ agrees. We swim back to shore with no more discussion.

Dripping water with every step I take toward the blanket, I inhale the sea air, then let it out. TJ tucks his arm around my waist, helping me up to our blanket.

"I'm sorry. I'm really drunk."

They look at each other, then back at me.

"Oh, Kai, I'm so worried about you," says Emily. Her voice sounds tired and sad. I know that feeling well.

TJ wraps the warm blanket around me. Emily adds her arm to my shoulder. The three of us stumble up to the Jeep soaking wet, carrying our dry clothes. Once inside, I lie across the backseat on the verge of passing out and tug my dress around my wet body. I stop fighting and just let go.

Chapter 10

Arbitrarily throwing an outfit together, no longer worried about my appearance, just trying to get through the day without collapsing under the weight of grief, I hear my parents arguing downstairs.

Again.

"Listen, we have to pick up the death certificate. We've dragged it on long enough," lawyer Dad states.

He's been trying to get my mom on board since we visited the funeral home. It's the only thing not checked off on the death list. But when she found it had been ruled a suicide — officially and forever — it was way too real.

"We are not keeping suicide on the death certificate, John."

"Marie" — his voice perturbed — "it's how she died whether we like it or not."

I feel my dad. Truth is truth.

"I want it changed. Mr. Barnes said he knows of other families who have requested that, especially when there's no insurance policy involved."

My mom has had this on a loop for days.

"It isn't going to change the result, Marie. Our daughter is dead. I don't give a damn about the paperwork. She's gone."

Her voice cracks. "Sheehans don't just kill themselves."

Breaking down, my dad corrects her. "They do now."

I hear his chair scrape the tile as he pushes it away from the table. His coffee cup lands with a bang in the stainless-steel sink. It's followed by the front door closing and the sound of his car roaring away.

* * *

Our drive to school is quiet. Mom has returned to her stylish, put-together self. Chanel suit, silk tank and tasteful accessories. I decide it's time to enlist her help.

"I need you to talk to Dad. I don't want to go right to college after senior year. I need this gap year. After all that's happened ..."

Mom keeps her eyes on the road. "It's not up for discussion, Kai. You aren't going. I agree with your father."

"It's one year, then I go to Florida State or wherever I get in. It's not that big of a deal."

"Then you don't need to go."

This is such bullshit. She's twisting my words around. "You know what I meant."

My tone has taken a sharp turn and it's bordering on indignant, which is fair. "I'm going. See if you can stop me."

Suddenly, I'm thrown back in my seat when my mother jerks the car and pulls over just outside the school drop-off. She turns to me and I swear she's spitting fire. "Your sister killed herself. Your father

90

and I are hanging on by a thread. You aren't moving five thousand miles away."

"It's a year from now."

"We don't care when it is."

"Half the yearbook staff is doing it." I keep at her.

"If they were all shaving their heads, would you want to do that, too?" she screams.

Such a Mom remark.

"It's not my fault that Jen killed herself. I shouldn't have to pay the price."

My mom's empty eyes match my heart. Still, I'm pissed off. I just want things to be normal again. And my parents won't even let that happen.

I open the door and don't look back. "See you later." I don't even wait for a response.

I walk toward the entrance of school clutching the SHEEHAN REALTY thermal coffee cup that's housing my much-needed caffeine fix. It counters the Vicodin crash. Jen's leftovers are saving me.

I'm greeted by the sound of the band in front of the school and a banner reminding everyone that there's a pep rally to send our basketball team off to sectionals. The cheerleaders are shouting and the sidewalk is bustling with students having fun. Normally, TJ and I would revel in this. Mock the jocks.

Not today. It's all too fucking much.

A text from Emily pops onto the screen of my phone.

Meet me outside the library

I ignore it.

The invisible walls are closing in on me. I manage to steer clear of Mr. Lancer, the assistant principal, who's patrolling the perimeter of the senior lot for pot smokers and rule breakers. Then I slip behind the bus line, leaving me a clear shot to freedom.

A few blocks away, I stop at the deserted Chevron station that's been boarded up for years. I sneak around back, out of sight, and dump my coffee in a trash can that's overflowing with candy wrappers and rancid food. I dig a room-temperature IPA out of my backpack, then swirl an ounce or two around to rinse the coffee mug out before I fill it with tepid golden-colored 5.2-percent alcohol. I toss the empty bottle with a perfect arc, watching it land on top of the fast-food bags in the trash can.

"Yes. Two points."

Make that six points: ditch successful, drink on, girl ready to roll. I am officially off the grid. Victory is mine.

Drinking my liquid courage, I stroll along a narrow sidewalk, careful not to be in the path my parents or friends might take this morning. A stray soda can litters my path so I make it my soccer ball for the duration of my expedition. I walk about a mile or so, struck by how little goes on this time of day on my side of town. I grin, thinking of how I used to kick rocks when Jen walked me to elementary school. She'd egg me on until my final kick that would hit the same trash can every day, then she'd pump her fist in the air, yelling, *Goal!* Right before she hugged me in front of my school and told me to have a good day. So long ago. Not a care in the world. I take a big swig, then jog across the street. It's in my sight, just a few hundred more feet. The cascading waterfall and old oak almost bring me peace until I remember who else is here.

For a long time and one more beer, I can only stand and stare at the outline on the lawn before me. The perfectly squared-off edges of the St. Augustine grass placed on top of the fresh grave. It's only been a few weeks though it seems like a hell of a lot more. There's still no headstone. My parents debated what it would say for days until my dad threw his hands up the air and screamed, "Do whatever you want!" to my mom. He didn't surface until the next morning.

I fixate on the small red plastic flag on the end of a smooth, rounded stick, signifying the dead body underneath.

My sister.

Collapsing under the weight of my heavy heart, I can't take my eyes off of her. Not really her, but the fresh sod on top of her. I can't turn off the ghastly thoughts running rampant through my mind. Are bugs eating away at her? Is she dry? Was Mr. Barnes telling the truth about the seal? What does she look like? Why did she do this?

It always comes back to that.

I try it out loud to see if that works.

"Why?" It's barely a whisper. No way she can hear me.

Louder, I try again. "Why?"

The waterfall seems louder, too. And the birds. And the wind. Like everything is amplified. Even the flapping of the flag planted on the grave. The sounds hammering my eardrums.

"In your letter you asked me to understand. The last favor you requested of me. And guess what? I just can't find my way to do that. Disappointing you is the last thing in the world I want to do but it's exactly what I'm doing. I don't know what else to do. You're the only one with the answer and you're … you're gone."

The best thing about cemeteries is that no one questions guttural sobbing. The woman cleaning the headstone of her loved one several yards away simply glances down as she scrubs, leaving me to wallow privately. I wipe my runny nose and eyes with the bottom of my Beatles T-shirt. It's pretty ripe.

A text from TJ interrupts me: *Where are you?*

Nowhere.

"Save me from this darkness. I just don't want to feel anymore. It's just too hard. Maybe this is how you felt? Was it? If it is, well … I want to be with you," I say quietly.

Lucky me: when I toss my phone into my backpack, I find another bottle of beer plus a bonus stray pill rolling around the bottom along with some quarters. Looks similar to a Vicodin, maybe a Norco. Don't really care what it is. After I pop it in my mouth and chug half the beer, I squish up my hoodie into a pillow. I position it next to the spot where Jen's head is resting, then crawl up next to her.

"I miss you," I manage before passing out.

* * *

Screaming voices and tugging on my sleeve jar me out of my slumber. I shield my face with my forearm but the sun's in my eyes and everything is blurry, I can't really focus. Someone holds something wet to my lips.

I manage a tiny sip. It's water, I think, and the moisture on my cracked lips soothes them. I squint, opening and closing my swollen eyes.

"… get her cleaned up … we need to take her home … she's a fucking mess." It's TJ's voice. I attempt to tell him I'm okay but I sound garbled.

"What did you take? Kai!"

"Shhhhh. Not so loud. Dead people are sleeping." Or at least that's what I think I say. Things are starting to come into focus. It's still blurry and my head is jumbled but that's definitely TJ poking through my backpack. And it's Emily holding the water bottle with her brow creased. I try to home in on what they're saying to each other.

"… her backpack … empty beer bottles. Jesus Christ, warm beer for breakfast … This is really bad, TJ … do you think she took any pills … what's happening here isn't just beer … call 911."

I can't have that. I search to find my voice.

"No! I'm fine."

"We have to sober her up, Em. She's circling the drain."

Through the haze I remember my parents have a dinner and won't be home until at least ten. Plenty of time.

"My parents are gone until way late," I manage. As my body is being hoisted up in the air, everything goes black.

* * *

The smell of spearmint and eucalyptus awakens me. TJ's favorite body spray. Startled, I make every effort to gather my wits about me. I rustle around and am met by the sight of my two best friends, who are vacillating between supremely pissed off and joyful to see me alive.

Emily comes at me ready for battle. "What the hell were you thinking?"

"I needed to talk to Jen, my parents don't understand me," I manage to whimper.

TJ sits on my bed next to me. I've never seen him look so helpless. He tugs on the leg of his board shorts.

"Kai, I was so worried. You were incoherent. Look at yourself. You haven't showered in who the fuck knows how long. You're on a slippery slope and falling down fast."

"Hey! Who the hell are you to judge me? You don't understand. No one understands," I retort.

"Stop playing that fucking card. You're right, we don't understand what it's like to lose someone we love, but you're here and we're here. Talk to us. Talk to somebody or you're gonna end up on the side of the road or worse," he shouts, pacing in front of me.

"TJ—" Emily starts. He rebuffs her.

Running his hands through his hair, his voice breaking, he mutters, "I can't handle the thought of losing you."

I know I sound weak but I muster up, "I really am sorry."

This time no one says it's okay.

"Don't let this shit happen again or I'll go to your parents myself," he says, anger creeping back in.

He hands me a bottle of water and some Advil. "Take these. Emily will make you a sandwich." Emily nods as she leaves my room.

Just the mention of food disgusts me and it's written all over my face. Before I can say a word, TJ gives me the *don't try it* look.

"It's not a request. Either you eat it or I call your mother."

"You sound like an asshole."

"If loving you makes me an asshole, so the fuck be it."

We sit glaring at each other for a few minutes, when Emily returns carrying a plate with a turkey-and-cheese sandwich and some potato chips. She hands it to me and sits at the foot of the bed with TJ, crossing her legs one over the other.

It takes a while but I swallow every morsel under their watchful eyes. So hard to chew when you're a sobbing wreck.

* * *

When I wake up, Duke is snoring next to me. A quick look at my phone: it's only seven o'clock. I have a slew of texts from my mom, TJ and Emily. I ignore all of them except for my mother.

We'll finish our talk tomorrow. Ok?

Yeah, Mom, sure. Home studying, have fun tonight.

Not a total lie. I really do need to study for my Trig test tomorrow. Sitting up, I realize that my head is in no space for that. I reach under the mattress for my pill stash and take a Vicodin to dull my throbbing head.

My gap-year packet is staring at me. I grab it, then lean down nose to nose with the dog. He opens his eyes and starts to thump his tail on the bed.

"Hi, buddy. I need to feed you. Let's get you some dinner." He cocks his head to the right as his ears stand at attention. The D-word perks him up as usual. Duke hurdles the bunched-up covers and races me down the stairs barking the entire way.

While he mows through his food, I go to my mom's office to leave her the packet from school about gap-year options. It's never too early. I'm not letting go. In the middle of her desk, I see a stack of mail. The envelope on top says *Jennifer Sheehan*. I thumb through the stack. All have her name on them. None will be opened by the recipient.

Clutching her mail like it might bring her back, I grab a bottle of bourbon out of a gift basket on Mom's floor. The baskets keep multiplying, and I could use a little shot to level me out. I know this would disappoint Em and TJ but WTF? They have no clue how hard this is.

"Bourbon?" I ask Duke, who is glued to me. I take his tail wag as a confirmation that this is a good idea, then proceed upstairs with the square bottle in hand.

The bourbon doesn't calm my nerves. The two Xanax I take do nothing. I run a bath hoping to wash away the despair coursing through my veins. Listening to the running water, I take Jen's last letter from the nightstand and skim it. I really don't need to look at it. The truth is, I've memorized every word.

Don't mourn me.

Like I can turn my heart on and off?

Celebrate the wonderful life you have ahead of you.

A life without you, Jen.

I can't get it out of my head now. Every word flashes rapidly in front of me, pulsating in my brain with no relief. After another mouthful of bourbon and my last Vicodin, I feel a sense of rage slam into me like a twelve-foot wave. I rant at my absent sister. At my life.

"Celebrate? Celebrate what, Jen? Your death?"

I flip out, losing control. With each sentence I get louder and louder. Madder and madder.

"You want me to turn my heart off, big sister? No problem. I'll turn my heart off, all right."

Mad.

Sad.

Resentful.

All colliding.

I storm over to my bed, facing the imposing headboard. This place used to be my refuge, the one place in the McMansion where I could lose myself in Jen's words and travels. I slash at a picture of me with Jen at Epcot Center. Her arms holding me so tight, so safe.

"What happened to you?"

I rip the postcards down and break nearly every framed picture in my path. I feel nothing. Nothing about the photo where we have on matching Florida State baseball hats. I throw that at the wall. Nothing about the photo where we parasailed in tandem. I smash the glass frame on the desk. Nothing about how all I wanted to do was be more like my beautiful, brown-haired, big-eyed sister in her senior picture.

Nothing!

A pair of scissors catches my eye, and with one swipe, I snatch them up and cut off a fistful of my hair.

Then another.

And another.

Clumps of my thick dark hair lie at the foot of my bed, covering the postcards and then some. I mindlessly strip my clothes off and rush back into the bathroom. The water pouring from the spigot is like a waterfall. Jen's waterfall — no! *Nothing*. I turn off the cascading water and lower my aching body into the warm bath. Resting my throbbing head on the back of the tub, I run my hand over my protruding ribs and try to push Jen's letter from my mind.

"I'm not scared of death. The alternative is too painful."

I get it, Jen. I get it.
Then I gently shut my eyes and the world out.

* * *

Bleary-eyed, prone on my bed, I think I hear the faint sound of my bedroom door opening, then closing with a click. I'm sure that's a dog barking nonstop. I slip the top sheet over my body against the slight breeze from my open window. It's so cold I'm shivering. The door handle turns, then the door opens but closes again. This time, I hear voices, but I don't see anyone through the impenetrable fog in my brain. The voices sound familiar. Mom? Dad? I catch every few sentences.

"What the hell were you thinking?"

"Jesus Christ, look at this mess."

A coffin appears before me. The lid opens, then closes. I try to check out what's inside but all I see is a black void. I hear my mother whisper to my dad.

"Let's calm down. Thank God TJ and Emily came to us."

"I know. I know. It's hard to be mad. She's in real trouble. But look at her hair."

"John, we have bigger problems than her hair."

The coffin lid creaks open once more, then slams shut, jarring me. I lift my head off the pillow ever so slightly and shake the cobwebs out of my foggy mind. It takes a minute but my mom's face slowly comes into focus.

I know better than to say anything. My life is stuck on pause.

It's so bright it hurts.

"Kai?" I hear my dad. "Try to sit up."

I see concern on their faces. I prop myself up on my elbow. "What time is it?"

"It's eight o'clock," Dad answers.

"Why is it so bright?" It's not registering with me.

"In the morning," he adds.

Doing the math, I know for sure I'm in a world of trouble. I've been asleep since some point yesterday. Shit.

Mom reaches for my hand. "Kai, when school is over next week, you're going to a camp in Georgia."

That gets my attention but quick.

"Georgia? To camp? I'm not going to camp. Ever. What am I, ten?" I sit straight up quickly but then wish I hadn't. All the blood rushes to my skull and I feel like I might be sick. Dad is standing next to Mom, all business. A united front.

"It's a grief camp for teens who have lost someone they love," she explains.

"A grief camp?" I yelp.

They don't flinch. Stone-cold resolve.

"One of my clients suggested it right after Jen died but we weren't sure about it. Until now," Mom explains.

"I'm not going anywhere to talk about Jen. I can handle it."

My dad pulls a bag of pot out of his pocket and lays it in front of me like an offering at an altar. "No, you can't."

"You searched my room?"

"We lost one child, we aren't about to lose another one. And it wasn't a question, Kai. It was a statement. You leave the day after school lets out next week. Your mom and I will drive you up."

I start to protest but I'm just too tired.

Tired of crying.

Tired of raging.

Tired of feeling alone.

Just so tired.

Chapter 11

When Dad wheels the Benz into a roadside restaurant in the middle of bumfuck nowhere, I raise my eyes. My earbuds have been pretty much jammed in my ears since we got in the car. Saying goodbye to TJ and Emily was a bitch but I squared things with them before I left. My first time away without any of my safety nets. No TJ. No Emily. No Jen.

"Let's stretch and grab a burger. This place is supposed to have the best cheeseburgers in Georgia," Dad throws out. He clocks my dubious look in the rearview mirror.

"It's true. One of the guys at my firm has a son who goes to Georgia Tech. He stops here on his way every trip."

Mom shakes her head but laughs. They're both trying so hard to be positive about this. A glimmer of lightness has made its way into them. I'm hoping for the same miracle.

The sign, FLO'S BURGERS, blinks in lime green even when the sun is shining and it's the middle of the day. Jen would love this place, I think. She lived for road trips to anything *Diners, Drive-Ins and*

Dives. I even know what she would order: cheeseburger, extra cheese, extra pickles, no onion. Extra-crispy fries. She loved the extras.

We find a red faux-leather booth way in the back. The chalkboard menu on the wall confirms it. It's pretty much burgers or cheeseburgers. Dad orders for us, then comes the silence that has become the norm since Jen died. No one knows what to say when we're all in one space. Here we are: no music, no work, just us.

Mom breaks the quiet. "Your dad and I really believe this is the right place for you to start the healing process, get rid of your anger." She's trying to sell me; it's what she does. I don't know.

"What if I promise to try harder?" I know I sound pitiful but I have to pull out all the stops. I do not want to talk about my sister with people I don't know.

My parents do what they do: side-eye each other hoping one of them will pick up the ball and run with it. It's Mom.

"Honey, we're afraid of what might happen to you if we don't get you help. We couldn't help Jen but we can help you."

I have no comeback for that. I can't keep lying. To them or to myself. Because it's true: I wanted to be with my sister.

"Trust me, leaving you at this camp is the last thing I want to do. But I know it's the only answer."

The thing about my mom is she believes in everything she sells and I believe in her because, right now, I have to.

"This is all they do. Help kids cope with devastating situations. Kai, you need this. We need this for you," Dad chimes in.

"I know," I say, subdued. It's what Jen would want me to do. In my head, I know she would want me to get my shit together and live my life, like she said in the letter. My heart is a whole different story. I can't let her go.

"I won't pretend to know why Jen thought that ending her life was her answer" — Dad's voice falters — "but I have all the confidence in the world that these people can help you navigate the waters of acceptance."

"Who are you?" I bust out, then cover with a giggle. But seriously, this is the kind of discussion I'd be having with my sister, certainly not with my father. At least the sister I thought I knew. Maybe my dad and sister had more in common than I realized.

I can tell my mom is trying not to cry. Finally she says what's on her mind.

"I'm sorry we've been so wrapped up in our own pain that we've been oblivious to yours."

The words almost get stuck in my throat. "It's okay." This time I mean it. They can't help themselves, let alone me. Maybe I do need to do this. I don't know if grief camp is the answer, but I'll try it.

For my mom, for my dad and for the sister I love the most.

* * *

As we cruise down the two-lane road in north Georgia that leads to grief camp, the only things I see are tractors, cows and horses. Then more cows. It's a far cry from Fort Lauderdale, and it's late afternoon by the time we arrive at The Tree House. Well named, it turns out. Trees as far as my eyes can see. Truly not much else.

Several families have beaten us here. Like robots, they appear to be going through the motions, unloading their cars, carrying duffel bags, like it's any other summer camp, except no one is smiling. All the faces are consumed with pain and uncertainty. With my nose glued to the back window, I start to have a mini–anxiety attack. Maybe a major one. The knots in my stomach tense while beads of sweat drip down my back.

"I can't do this," I tell my parents. No way.

I hear the doors click open. My parents are blatantly ignoring me. Damn, damn, damn.

"You'll be okay, Kai." Mom says the words, but her voice sounds a lot like the freaked-out one in my head.

Before I can continue to protest, Dad opens my door and we're greeted by a fresh-faced girl wearing a big smile and a canary-yellow T-shirt that says *The Tree House Staff* on the front over the upper-left pocket. This leaves me no choice but to climb out of buttery-soft seats into the unknown.

"Hi, I'm Alison. I'm one of the orientation leaders."

My dad throws his hand out right away, ever the gentleman. "John Sheehan. This is my wife, Marie, and our daughter, Kai."

"I'm so very sorry for your loss. I know this must be an extremely difficult time for all of you," she says. It's the millionth time I've heard it … but the first time I've heard it like this. Like it's minus the usual underlying sorrow. Like there's no pity. Like it's … crap, I can't overthink this. It's … just enough.

Alison rattles off information quickly and concisely. "You'll be sharing a cabin with Cass, another girl your age. She hasn't arrived yet. Orientation starts in a little less than an hour. There's plenty of time to look around, maybe take a walk down to the lake once you drop your stuff and get settled." The polka-dot bow on her ponytail distracts me. It bops up and down as she talks and leads us down a well-traveled path of dirt and leaves. We pad around the great outdoors surrounded by the tallest evergreens I've ever seen. Majestic statement makers, unlike the palm trees of South Florida. My dad in his starched chinos, my mom with her diamond earrings ... *out of place* is an understatement.

"This is your cabin," Alison tells us.

You know when you're about to drop *what the fuck* but your inner ten-second rule takes over? That's happening right now as I assess my new home. "Stay positive," I mutter to myself. I traipse up the weathered wooden steps. An etched sign to the right of the doorway says CABIN 2.

Jesus Christ.

Reminders everywhere, even at grief camp. I thrust my elbow out, jabbing my mother, who sees the number two and knows, like I do, that it's Jen's old apartment number. No words needed. She nudges me gently forward through the entry. Since I've never shared a room in my entire life or ever gone camping, the sparse accommodations are a stunner. Two twin beds flush against tan walls with plain pine nightstands between them. So monochromatic and slight. To make matters worse, the mattress is covered in plastic.

"Worried we'll wet the bed?" I ask, attempting a touch of levity in this impossible situation.

Alison doesn't miss a beat, leading me to believe I'm not the first camper to note this. "It's a law. Keeps bedbugs away."

Now *that* thought will stay with me for the next twenty-nine nights.

Matching pine dressers on one side of the room, industrial desks on the other, with a couple of uncomfortable-looking chairs slid under them. Distressed-wood floors covered in a paisley rug that's tattered on the outer edges. A miniature tweed couch that has certainly seen better days. This place could pass for juvie. Dad hauls in my duffel bags and sets them down in the middle of the room.

"If you need anything while you're getting settled in, my cell number is on this sheet," Alison says, handing my mom a detailed map of the grounds. "Make yourself at home. See you in the main house at three."

And then we're alone.

I check out the hovel. "It's so cramped." These new living quarters of mine could fit into our family room with plenty of space to spare.

"You probably won't spend a lot of time in here," Dad says, like he meant to say, *shouldn't spend a lot of time in here.*

"Which bed do you want?" Mom starts unpacking the sheets. Right. Get on with it. Power through.

"The one under the window," I say, kicking into action with her. "At least there's a view." We both semi-laugh, seeking any relief from the tension that's flooding this place. I mean, there's nothing out there but a stack of wooden produce boxes, some random hoses and a couple of trails in the dirt.

She tosses the fitted bottom sheet in my direction so that we can start to make the bed. We had to buy twin-size color-block sheets at Bed, Bath and Beyond since I haven't had a bed this small in forever. It's like a miniature candy bar, you get just enough but not really. At our house, we graduate bed sizes every five years or so. I hijacked Jen's king-size when she went off to college.

Another reminder.

When we get to the top sheet, Mom takes over, spreading it evenly across the bed, tucking the end of the sheet between the mattress and noisy box spring. I watch as she makes her way to the top of the bed, adjusting the sheet, yanking it taut. She folds the corners at the foot of the bed with military precision. I can't believe what I'm witnessing, and neither can my dad, who's pretending not to watch. You could bounce a quarter off that sucker. She hasn't made my bed in years but she's making sure this bed is perfect.

"You know it's never going to look like that again, right?" I tease.

I begin to unpack my things.

I reach into the bottom of the linens duffel and tug on the chocolate throw. I set it at the foot of the bed, doubling it up on top of my sheets. Mom dots her eyes with a Kleenex. She's been keeping them in every pocket since Jen died.

"I'm glad you brought that with you. Jen loved it," she comments as I bunch it up just right.

Digging into Jen's backpack, I notice the few stashed Xanax that my parents didn't find. Wisely, I hid them in a zippered pocket while I was packing. No way I could deal with this without a bit of synthetic assistance. I unearth Hershel and am transported back to dropping Jen off at the Miami International Airport when she went to Europe. She had this same bag slung over her shoulder, ready to tackle the world. I start to slide out a few of the postcards that weren't lost in the whole I'm-ripping-my-room-to-shreds episode. I can't help but smile when I see one with my favorite book cover on it: *Charlotte's Web*. The first time Jen read me the book I was so upset that Charlotte died, she held me for hours until I fell asleep.

I can't bear to turn it over. Seeing her handwriting now is just too raw.

I get Hershel situated, then carefully take out Jen's shirt and unwrap the family photo I packed. I didn't smash this one, thank God or whoever. It's in the seashell picture frame I made with Jen's help. Seeing what I have, Dad grabs Mom's hand. I display the photo on the bare pine table next to my bed, where I can see it every morning when I wake up. Fluffing Jen's shirt, I toss it across the headboard for now.

"That was a great trip, wasn't it?" Dad asks, trying to make conversation.

"It really was," I whisper. "We're never going to be able to do that again."

"We'll make new memories, I promise," he says, almost mumbling.

"Kai, come sit down, I have something for you," Mom says.

She reaches inside her purse and ferrets out a shiny red-and-green-covered package. Santa and Rudolph in June? WTF?

Mom blinks. "When we went through Jen's closet, we found Christmas presents for each of us."

Blindside. "She really thought of everything, didn't she?"

"Your dad and I thought this might be the place for you to open it whenever you're ready."

"Did you guys open yours?" Not that it makes any difference.

"Not yet."

"I can't do this right now." I sigh, cramming the gift inside the backpack, under my books, iPad, journal and candy.

Lots of candy.

Mom and I start puttering around the room, mindlessly unloading the rest of my things. Clothes. Books. Shoes.

When I throw my duffel on the worn couch, I spot one of those crocheted quotes hanging on the bare vanilla wall. Crochet on the walls? That's something Nana would have. I start to roll my eyes but then I read the words.

Only when it's dark enough, you can see the stars.

It can't get much darker. I've never needed to see the light of a star so badly.

Ever.

* * *

Tucked between my parents, listening to the ground rules, I check my phone every few minutes for status updates. I need a lifeline from home right now.

"Breakfast starts at seven thirty, your group therapy is at nine," I hear. Oh, God. Group therapy. It's really happening. There aren't enough pictures on Instagram to make that better.

"Lunch is at noon. Dinner at six. Lights out at eleven. Your afternoons will be up to your counselors. Your packets include a map of hiking trails and a list of emergency contacts," announces Alison, who's up on a small stage with a microphone and a clipboard.

With the obligatory welcome and orientation nearing a close, anxiety spreads over my body like poison ivy.

"Families, if you have any more questions, the counselors will be available out front to assist you," Alison continues. "Kids, once you've said your goodbyes, we'll get together in the recreation hall next door so you can meet your groups." According to my welcome packet, my therapy group consists of four other teenagers — three guys and the girl who is supposed to be my bunk mate. I will be oversharing my deepest feelings with this group of strangers?

No, thanks.

Then I remember: Crap, I made a promise to make an effort. I'm stuck with all this camp BS for a whole month. It stretches ahead of me like a century. Perhaps there will be s'mores.

All the families, including mine, make a mass exodus to their cars for a final farewell. My mom steers clear of eye contact, trembling as she marches.

"Please don't leave me here. I can't talk about her with strangers. They didn't know her," I plead.

The crease between my dad's eyes deepens, and he grabs the collar of his shirt. I can sense his emotions are ripping through him but at least he answers me. "Kai, your mom and I don't want you ever to leave our sight. But we can't give you the kind of help you need right now. These people are experts. I can't tell you how much I wish it could be us helping you through this."

I run into his arms like I used to do before work took over his life and Jen's dying took over mine. I allow my father to really comfort me for the first time since the day Jen died. When we break apart, he brushes the drops from his cheek, then wipes away mine with his big Daddy-size thumb.

"Trust me on this. She loved you more than her own life. She wants you to be okay."

His argument is solid — arguing is what he does for a living. Still, how does he really know? "Her exact words to me in my letter," he reveals.

"I promise to try," I manage to say.

Watching Dad's Mercedes creep down the roadway, getting smaller and smaller until it disappears, I brace myself for the unfamiliar. I am filled with dread.

Chapter 12

Any other day, I'd be at least a few vodka shots plus a Vicodin or two into it. Not today. I have some time to kill before I greet my strangers at the assembly. I'm sprawled on my bed, staring at the knotty wood ceiling, thinking about the last few weeks of hazy hell. This must be what rock bottom looks like.

I thumb the Favorites on my phone and tap the second name. Jen's is first and I'm not deleting it. Not even two rings and I see a face so elated that it instantly assuages my fear. TJ's mug fills my Facetime screen.

"I'm so happy to see you," he says.

"I'm happier than you, trust me. Look at this place." I wave the phone around the room for a panoramic view.

"It's not that bad. I know it'll suck at first, but then it won't."

"How can you be so sure?"

"Because that's the way things go." He's quiet for a minute. "If Em and I could have helped you, we would have. We did as much as we could."

"Like telling my parents on me?" I take a little cheap shot.

"I have no regrets. I thought we were past this. The three of us are a team. You would've done the same thing if it was one of us. You're going to be surrounded by kids who are going through the exact same thing as you."

I do know why he turned me in.

"You know I'm not a big sharer." I plead my case.

"Get out of your comfort zone," he chides.

"So not easy for me and you know it."

He softens, his puppy-dog eyes reaching out to me. "I have faith in you."

"Love you, TJ." It's all I've got at the moment.

"Same."

The next thing I see is his lips kissing the phone screen. He's a dork but he's my dork.

"Time to go to meet my group." I am terrified.

"Be open. Text whenever you can."

* * *

Left foot.

Right foot.

With much hesitation, I thrust open the pea-green double doors of the log cabin rec room, desperation hanging in the air like cheap perfume. Pool tables, a Ping-Pong table and vending machines decorate the otherwise ordinary space. The tan-ish walls are covered with pictures of campers who've come before me. One for every year, like in the yearbook. And they're smiling. How is that even possible? I comb the cavernous recreation room for Group Five, grateful it isn't Group Two. According to the numbered tables, there are six groups. Some of them are long cafeteria tables designed to fit more kids. Others are round with five or so plastic off-white chairs. Looks like there's about fifty of us altogether. Different ages, different sizes, different colors. One common denominator.

A chipped sign with a bright white 5 in the center peeks out from behind a post in the far back corner. The other strangers in my group are already parked there in dead silence. The first one to catch my eye is a rosy-cheeked girl wearing an embroidered dress and Toms shoes, nervously twirling her spiky jet-black hair. She's the lone girl, so I'm thinking she must be my roommate. The Toms tell me she's got a social conscience, so how bad can she be? The grungy-looking guy to her left, wearing ripped jeans and an attitude for days, with longish dark black hair peeking out from under his beanie, has his arms crossed, avoiding eye contact with the others. Not so sure about him. His feet are propped up on the chair next to him, the red shoelaces of his work boots untied. He looks more apathetic than me.

Next to beanie guy, a younger, sweet-faced kid with flaxen hair and freckles, wearing some kind of silver necklace, has his knees tucked up to his chin. His white Vans knockoffs have seen better days.

Like all the people who are stuck here.

Across the room, I spot quite possibly the hottest guy I've ever laid eyes on and he's headed my way. His chiseled face and athletic build lead me to peg him as a jock. I know I'm stereotyping but I'm okay with that. I can use the distraction. Eye candy at grief camp? "Sorry I'm a little late. My mom had a hard time leaving me," he announces. How is he so loose and chipper?

116

Beanie boy throws him a look of disgust, then goes back to staring at his bootlaces. As I approach the table, I catch the eye of an older, olive-skinned guy with a buzz cut just about to sit down. He's wearing surfer shorts and a Tree House T-shirt, carrying a stack of books.

"Hey. Group Five?" he asks. I nod as I slide out a chair and plop onto it. The only thing on the table is a plastic cup filled with pens. I have a bad feeling about that. He sets the books down next to him.

"Hi, everyone. I'm Marco Esposito, your grief counselor. I'll be leading your group for your duration here. Today will be quick, informal, break the ice a little. Get to know one another before we officially kick off group therapy tomorrow. Did you all bring the stuff on the list we sent?"

We all grumble yes.

When my parents dropped that bomb on me, I lost it. They didn't care. So I gathered up pictures of Jen and all the other items required for my stay here.

"We'll use them for some of the exercises you'll be doing over the next few weeks."

What was not on the list was that fact, though maybe I should have guessed. Show-and-tell at grief camp.

"So ... why don't we go around the table? Tell us your name and something about yourself."

No one steps up to the plate. There's a lot of looking up, down and sideways. Marco takes the hint and the lead.

"I'll start. I'm twenty-two. I just graduated from UCLA with an International Business degree. The first time I came here, I was thirteen. My mom was diagnosed with end-stage breast cancer when

I was twelve. When she died, my dad left. He couldn't handle having kids without a mother to do all the work. My older brother, Hector, who pretty much raised me, brought me here. It saved my life," he shares, with an emphasis on the last four words.

I most definitely do not want to follow that. Too bad; he turns to me and throws me a wink. I get it: my turn.

"Kai Sheehan. I'm sixteen. I have a four-year-old golden retriever named Duke. I miss him already." I twist the sleeve of my Rolling Stones T-shirt nervously, hoping my voice isn't shaky. That's all I'm offering up.

I pivot toward the freckled-faced younger kid who has been nonstop quiet-crying since we all sat down. He's slight and so frail looking. His camo utility shorts are baggy, not in a trendy way, and his hair looks like it hasn't been combed in days.

He stumbles through. "Ben Ellis. My mom and dad were killed in a car accident. My little brother is in a coma." Teardrops roll down his face, and we all kind of look away, not wanting to embarrass him.

And this isn't even "group" group. I'm never going to last here.

My roommate is up next, fiddling with her hair as she talks. "Hi. I'm Cass Salisbury, I write songs and sing in a band." Her body is birdlike but her mouth is full, her cheeks as rosy as Braeburn apples. The jet-black shiny hair helps with the rocker image. That and she's really pretty without a stitch of makeup other than ruby-red lipstick.

"That's way cool." That slips right out of my mouth and Cass half smiles. Beanie guy flips me the death stare. Mr. Hot Guy steps up.

"Jack Sumner. I play football for my high school. That's about it." I knew it. The cuts on his biceps and the way he fills out his

New York Yankees gray-and-blue T-shirt support the football stuff, but his suave demeanor … there's more to this guy than *that's about it*. I catch him swinging his foot from side to side. More nervous than he likes to admit, I think.

Mr. Apathy yanks his purple-and-gray Neff beanie down to just above the top of his bushy eyebrows. A few pieces of his dark hair sneak over the collar of his loose-fitting V-neck navy striped shirt. A total rebel. Looking up at us, his fiery blue eyes catch me off guard. "Graham Nelson. I don't want to be here." I sympathize with him, but that is kind of rude considering the rest of us played along.

Marco jumps in to ease the tension. "It's okay, Graham, I understand. I didn't want to be here on my first day either. It'll get easier."

Graham returns to brooding while Marco goes over some of the stuff they already covered in the orientation.

"Every day will be structured so that you have activities, group therapy and some free time. The lake is beautiful this time of year; take advantage of it. One quick thing before I let you go."

He passes out blank sheets of paper.

"You'll be keeping daily journals beginning today. The lake is a great place to write, at least it was for me. Still is."

The word *journal* lands like a thud with Graham. He's clearly seething, tapping his forefinger on the wood table. Ben raises his hand.

"Go ahead, Ben," Marco says, "you don't need to raise your hand. Jump in anytime. That goes for all of you."

"How do we journal? I've never done anything like this before. The only things I write are math problems I'm solving."

I'm so not journaling for anyone to read. No fucking way am I sharing my thoughts with anyone, let alone a bunch of people I've just met.

"There's no right or wrong way to journal. If you want, you can start every entry with 'Today I ...' then take it from there. Write down your feelings, your memories of your loved one, pretty much anything you'd like."

Graham mutters something unintelligible.

"Before you take off for the night, we'll do a simple exercise to get you accustomed to it. Write down a few adjectives that describe how you feel now. Don't overthink it. Just jot down whatever comes to mind."

So that's what the paper is for.

Marco notices how pissed off Graham is. He's given his laces a rest but now he's flicking his middle finger on the table so hard that it sounds like a drum.

"Put your rage on the page." Marco prods Graham.

I stare at the words that I'm not sharing: *Depressed. Tired. Scared.* I turn the paper over. Not taking any chances.

"Believe it or not, writing your feelings on paper will make it easier to say them out loud," Marco professes.

Then he passes out the books that he brought. Blank journals. Sneaky bastard.

"So it's cool if I write a song about my grandma or draw something?" asks Cass.

"Absolutely. As long as it's something. Every day for the next twenty-nine that you are here."

Christ.

"What if we don't want to do it?" I question him. I know it's argumentative, but I didn't know this was part of the deal. I mean, I don't want to be forced to write my feelings down where anyone could find them. All eyes are on me.

Marco spells it out for us. "The journaling is designed to help you deal with what you are going through by articulating yourself, so it's not an option. What is optional is sharing what you write with anyone else. That's up to you."

"Definitely not doing that," I confirm much louder than I would have liked.

Marco pushes his chair back from the table, making an awful screeching sound like fingernails on a blackboard. "Okay, guys, you have about an hour before dinner. I'm in the counselors' cabin, next to the dining hall, if you need anything. My door is always open."

As we all get up, Cass grabs my arm. "Want to go down to the lake?"

"Why not?" I start to invite the guys but they all beat it out of here the second Marco moved his chair. We start walking toward the lake, leaves crunching underneath our feet. I'm not used to that sound.

"I guess we're roommates. That's cool," I offer up, trying to share more than the fact that I have a dog.

"So my story," she begins, like we're old friends. "My grandmother died a few weeks ago and I completely lost it, I just couldn't function. I was so depressed, I couldn't pull myself out of the funk I was in. I couldn't get past the finality of it all." I nod and listen, completely understanding what she's talking about. I resist the urge to yell, *Same!* I reserve that word for TJ, it's our thing.

"My grandma pretty much raised me and my brothers and sister. When I was eight, my dad left one day to buy beer and never came back. Mom loves meth more than us. It would be ridiculously cliché if I was watching some lame movie of the week, but it's the ugly truth. Grandma took us all in. Now she's gone."

"I'm so sorry. Where's your mom now?"

"With my siblings. She's the one who sent me here. She went to rehab last year. So far, so good, but I don't trust her. This is her third time. She's not the strongest person in the world. She always has an excuse, 'It was just a slip.' Some crap like that. Each time she gets clean, she pours on all kinds of promises that she never keeps."

"Third time's the charm?" I try.

"Maybe."

"Don't give up on her."

Cass stops, cocking her head. She's not sure about me, I can tell. Shaking it off, she takes that tidbit and files it somewhere, then conveniently changes the subject. Heavy feelings are hard.

"I love your name," she remarks, trying to keep the conversation going. Both of us treading water, or at least I am. Cass seems like more of an open book than I will ever be. Such a casual manner about the way she moves and speaks.

"Thanks. Kai means 'sea' in Hawaiian. I was born in Honolulu."

"That's so cool. I've never been outside of Trenton until now," she confesses sheepishly.

"My dad's law firm moved our family out there for a year so he could run their satellite office for a big case they were trying when my mom was pregnant with me. My sister helped name me. She loved the ocean, we went to the beach almost every weekend growing up," I share.

"She sounds pretty great."

"Yeah, she really was." *Was.* That word stings when I say it out loud for the first time to a person I met less than an hour ago.

"Sorry," she replies. She knows that my sister is the reason I'm here. She speaks my language.

We stroll in silence to the water's edge and sit down on a large, jagged rock in the shade. Birds seem to be singing to each other, back and forth. That doesn't happen in Fort Lauderdale unless you own parakeets. Which we don't.

"Check it out!" Cass points to a fish jumping out of the middle of the water and plopping back in with a splash. "You don't see that kind of thing in New Jersey."

"No fish there?"

"Only frozen fish sticks. One of my grandmother's favorite things to make for us. Every Friday. Always with Tater Tots."

"Sorry ..."

"Don't worry about it. What I have learned the past few weeks is that nearly everything reminds me of her."

I know how that feels. "Good to know it isn't just me."

A cacophony of insects fills the air, creeping me out, but it doesn't take away from the beauty of the sun shining on the lake, making each ripple from the swimming fish dance on top of the water.

"Jack is like crazy hot, right?" Cass asks, chuckling, changing the subject.

I know this is not the place to take applications for boyfriends, but it's true that his hot factor is off the charts. It's the first time in quite a while that no one is talking about death or feelings so I welcome it with open arms.

"Yeah, I noticed. He seems to be in better spirits than the rest of us," I say.

"My money is on him being a hider. You know, together on the outside, disguising his hurt," she theorizes.

"Still, he's so hot, it hurts." I scare up a laugh.

"Bad that we're even checking him out at grief camp?" asks Cass.

Maybe. Maybe not. I shrug. "It's a nice change of pace."

Cass gets up, rummaging through the evergreen needles for something. "Ah, this is it." She opens her hand, showing me a rock that's kind of on the flat side, about five inches long. Staring down the lake like it's the enemy, she cocks her arm sideways and lets the rock rip across the top of the water, skipping at least four times.

"Impressive."

"The one thing my dad taught me before he left."

Wow. This is the first time in weeks I've been completely sober. I think back to my dad. He would never leave me. I hope I can do this.

Chapter 13

When I hear Marco announce karaoke after dinner, I wince.

"Just no," I fume.

Cass is delighted. "Come on. This will be so fun. We should sing a duet." That will happen the day after never.

Not sure how the guys feel about it, but when Graham wads up his napkin and throws it on his untouched meat loaf, I think I have at least one ally.

Alison coaxes a few of the younger kids to get up when she starts the music to "Let It Go." I'm stunned to see how many people join in and are singing along, including Cass. The boys and I are solid in our stonewalling of this activity, though maybe Ben is humming.

Graham leans into me. "Great. Now this will be stuck on repeat in my head for the rest of the night."

"My ears are so mad right now," I add, making him laugh.

The chorus starts, and no one but me and my boys are holding back. Everyone else is singing at the top of their lungs and some are even dancing.

If I rolled my eyes any harder, I'd give myself a black eye.

Jack scoots his chair closer to me. "The song. Really?"

That gives me the giggles.

"Think we can ditch outta here?" *Please say yes.*

He bobs his head to the left. "There's a back door." I see the EXIT sign and slowly slip out of my seat. Jack taps Graham. The three of us slink out as the next song starts with Cass at the microphone. "Summer Lovin'."

Good God.

* * *

Curled up in the corner of the couch with my earbuds in, I reach for Jen's throw to cover my feet. A card drops out of one of the folds. There's a *K* scrawled on the envelope. The flap isn't sealed. My fingers shake as I tug on the card, recalling the contents of the last envelope I opened. The front of the card brings a ray of light to my face. A golden retriever who could easily pass as Duke with three bright yellow tennis balls crammed in his mouth. Inside, the five words I read turn me to mush: *You can do this. Dad.*

Brushing the happy from my eyes, I open the dreaded journal. Cass is fast asleep, or pretending to be. I start to scribble randomly as the beat of Keane keeps me company. I take Marco's suggestion and start with something simple like my day. Ease into things.

Today ...
     Was my first day at grief camp and the name certainly does it justice. There's grief everywhere. It comes in all

shapes, sizes, colors and ages. It doesn't discriminate. They need another name for this place. I doubt any other "camps" have a never-ending supply of Kleenex, let alone try to pass off therapy as an activity. I wonder how many kids are here because of suicide, like me. My guess is zero. My group seems all right, it was like the first day of class at a new school where everyone's all shy and nervous. It's unusual, though. When I think of my group, I think about Emily, TJ, Kate and Bridget. We all share the same interests. Here it's a whole different animal. Guys like Ben at my school hang out together, not with jocks like Jack.

There's a lot of people here, just not the one person I want. And that person will never be here again.

My sister wasn't a liar yet she sat right across from me shoveling pasta into her mouth, laughing at my jokes, then went home and killed herself. That's two-faced if you ask me.

I can't believe I just wrote that.

I want the muffled whispering to stop. I want to stop seeing pity in people's eyes when they glance in my direction. I am tired of casseroles and cupcakes. My life is split in two: the before and the after. Maybe my sister knew something I didn't know.

You can't feel pain if you're dead.

* * *

The next morning, I take a quarter of a Xanax just to take the edge off before texting Emily.

Hey Em, my first real group therapy session is in, like, five minutes. I hope mediocre waffles and undercooked bacon don't set the tone for the day or I'm screwed.

I'm with you in spirit. I know it's your first step to healing. E

How do you know?

I just do. Xo

I muster up my courage as I slip the phone in my pocket and pray this won't be a total disaster. Baring my soul to strangers isn't really my thing. On the plus side, Marco picked a wooded, secluded spot for our group so we won't be on display for the entire camp to witness our breakdowns. Cass and I traipse through the woods and find that we aren't the first ones to arrive.

Jack is already leaning against one of the endless pine trees with his hands folded neatly behind his head, showing off his biceps and hotness in a dark green tank top and mesh gym shorts, with black-and-red leather high-tops. Every move he makes causes a ripple effect on his muscular arms. I get a little flustered imagining the abs hidden underneath his shirt. Too bad TJ isn't here, he'd have something to say about this. I start to text him a picture but then I remember rule number one: no phones during group. As I squelch that idea, Jack waves at us.

"Hey, how's it going?" I call in a high-pitched voice that comes out of nowhere. Cass just throws up her hand with some indifference. Exactly what I should have done instead of sounding moderately geeky. Who am I kidding? A lot geeky.

Marco greets us. "Good morning." He's juggling a soccer ball that has phrases written in every section of the ball. Pretty sure I see the words *Best memory* in one of the marked boxes. This causes me to fidget and nervously scratch my chin.

Cass and I both turn when we hear a branch snap and rustling behind us. It's not a wild animal, just Graham, looking as surly today as he did yesterday. I'm guessing that when he sees the word ball, his mood won't improve. At least he nods to acknowledge our presence. His shorts show off athletic legs that were hiding under his jeans yesterday.

Ben tags along, closely trailing him, hands buried so deep in his pockets I worry his fingers may rip through his shorts.

Upbeat, Marco explains what we're doing. "Okay, guys, we're gonna sit in a circle over here. It's called the circle of trust. While we are here, you can talk about anything with no judgment from the group. I won't share anything with your families. This is a safe zone for you and your feelings."

Oh boy. I don't know.

"Jesus Christ, are you kidding?" Graham blurts. He turns beet red when he realizes he actually said the words out loud.

Marco raises that ominous soccer ball above his head, causing my angst level to skyrocket. "We're going to use this soccer ball for our first activity. It's called Thumb Ball."

He twirls it around, revealing all the words. I catch a few as he twirls it. *Favorite day. Best present. Favorite activity. Memorable moment. Characteristic you loved. Vacation memory.* Nothing I want to tell him.

"We'll toss the ball around the circle. When you catch the ball, you'll look under your right thumb to see which phrase is closest to your finger and discuss it. After you share, throw the ball to someone else in the circle. Today's subject is your loved one who died."

I'm back to praying to the God I don't believe in. *Please do not let that sucker come flying my way first.* That's the crucial thing: not to me.

129

Graham checks the soles of his Vans, flipping the laces around. Gnawing the loose skin on the knuckle of his right hand.

Marco whips that sucker straight to Cass. I suspect he guesses she's the least terrified in the group. And what do you know? She catches it like a champ. Cass lifts up her thumb. "'Favorite activity.'"

"Before you begin, tell the group who you lost," Marco interrupts.

I knot up so tightly that my shoulder cracks from the tension. I'm pretty sure everyone hears it. Graham bristles and starts kicking around the evergreen needles. Ben just starts sniffling. Jack acts like he's game for anything. Ever the cool one.

For me, this is going to be a bitch. I have to say my sister died — killed herself — to people who don't know me and who didn't know her. They might judge her. Or me.

Cass speaks up. "My grandmother died a few weeks ago." Her voice gets a little shaky as she reads the phrase under her thumb again: "'Favorite activity.'"

Inhale. Exhale. I cross my arms to match my legs, which are twisted like a pretzel.

"My grandma used to make chocolate-chip cookies with my siblings and me for special occasions. Only her idea of a special occasion was just about anything. Like, it was a sunny day, or it didn't snow. She liked to make it a big deal and it was. Every single time." She grins ever so slightly before the doldrums creep in. "I haven't had a single cookie since she died."

No cookies and losing the person who's been like a mother to her.

She throws the ball across the circle at Graham. "My twin brother was killed by a drunk driver," he mumbles.

Oh, I think. That sucks.

"'Favorite food,'" he mutters. Graham moves his heel from side to side, digging in the dirt. He tugs on the neck of his T-shirt.

Marco notices his overwhelming discomfort. "Just give it a shot."

Graham bends forward and grabs his foot like he's talking to it, avoiding eye contact with the group. I don't blame him.

In a strained, quavering voice, he answers, "Pizza. It was the only thing Justin would eat when we were kids and it stayed his favorite right up until the crash. We went to Luigi's right after our lacrosse game. Like always."

I notice his T-shirt says *It takes balls to play Lacrosse*. TJ would absolutely love that.

"It was our ritual. He could eat an entire pepperoni pizza by himself. Afterward, a bunch of our friends decided to go to the beach for a bonfire. I told him to go ahead without me. I had homework to do. We did everything together. Just not that night."

His voice shivers. We all watch his tough exterior shatter like a mirror hitting the pavement. The trickle of tears down his tanned face slashes at me. I raise my eyes at Marco, who gives me the okay signal with a slight nod of his head. I slowly get up and sidle next to Graham, offering what's left of the Kleenex I've been wadding up since I sat down. He buries his face in his hands — right after he rolls the ball in my direction.

Ugh.

I think I hear my heart pounding against my chest. I cough, clear my throat and forge ahead. "My sister, Jen, died. Well, more like, she committed suicide. It was just a normal Tuesday. And then it wasn't."

There it is, out in the open for everyone to hear. The S-word. I despise it but I can't exactly leave it out. I lift my twitching right thumb, terrified to see the words that lie beneath.

"'Vacation memory,'" I gasp. There's not enough Xanax in the world to make this okay.

"I have so many," I say, racking my brain for a stand-out moment. Finally one pops into my head. "We went to a dude ranch in Wyoming for a family trip when I was thirteen and Jen was nineteen. She was home from college for summer break. I was terrified of horses. Still am. I'm okay if they don't move but it's the whole moving thing that doesn't work for me. When it came time for us to go on our first ride, I totally lost it. Everyone was saddled up, waiting to explore, while I just stood there crying. Jen didn't miss a beat. She jumped down off her horse, coaxed me into mounting my horse, then put her foot in the stirrups and joined me, taking the reins as she closed her arms around me. She told me she'd always have my back." Everyone nods encouragingly before I deliver the kicker. "She lied."

I can't help the waterworks that follow. Graham offers me a knowing look and chucks the ball to Ben.

Ben traps it between his chest and hand, yanking it down to his lap. "You already know both of my parents died," he says, twitching. He picks up his thumb.

"'Best present.'" He breathes a noticeable sigh of relief. His chest heaves as he begins.

"That's easy. Every birthday starting from kindergarten on I asked for a kitten and got the same answer over and over, *no*. Then out of nowhere, I came home from school last year and there was a black-

and-white ball of fur in my laundry basket staring up at me. Someone at my mom's work found a box of kittens that were abandoned at the Laundromat so she took one home for me. As soon as I picked him up, he started purring and curled up under my chin. It was like he was destined to be mine. Toby is all I have left of them."

Jesus Christ.

Ben heaves the soccer ball to Jack, who's waiting with his arms spread wide.

"My father was killed in a roadside explosion in Afghanistan." He's totally calm and composed. He lifts up his thumb. "'Last time you were together.'"

He swallows so hard that his Adam's apple vibrates.

"We were at a hangar in a remote section of our local airport before he deployed. Me, my dad and my mom. An enormous military transport plane sat in the middle of the tarmac. All of the soldiers' families were inside saying their goodbyes. I remember thinking of how sterile and cold it was in there. Just a big old room filled with fear. So many little kids sending their fathers or mothers off to battle yet still waving glittery signs saying 'I Love My Dad' and stuff that I thought was ridiculous. I was so pissed off that he was fighting a stupid war I didn't agree with that I acted like a total dick. I didn't tell him that I would really miss having him cheer at my games. I finally landed the starting quarterback position at my high school but the guy who taught me to throw will never see me start. I didn't tell him that I loved him or anything else."

A throaty sob creeps into his voice. "And I'll never have that chance again."

So intense.

Marco breaks the silence. "Okay, guys, I know how tough it is to talk about your loved ones in front of a group you've just met. Right now, your emotions are raw. But exercises like this are designed to help you get the words out," he tells us. "It will be a little easier every time."

I rub my eyes, willing myself not to break down again. My eyes take a loop around my circle. So much pain.

My group.

I'm bracing myself for another exercise when Marco announces some good news. "I think this is enough for our morning session. How about a little extra free time before lunch?"

A collective sigh of relief fills the air.

"Did everyone write in their journals?" Marco asks.

All of us nod though I'm not sure if everyone's telling the truth.

"After lunch we'll meet at the arts-and-crafts zone. It's an outdoor area behind the dining room.

"Arts and crafts?" grumbles Graham.

"That sounds fun," Cass snipes at him, trying to return to her spunky self.

Arts and crafts were my thing with Jen. I'm so with Graham on this. His eyes catch mine, blinking in total agreement.

We all rise to get the hell out of there. Fast.

"Hold up, everyone," says Marco. "Before we go, I need you all to join hands. This is called the squeeze. At the end of every session, we'll do this as a reminder that you are not alone."

Okay, this is a little much. I take Graham's shaking hand in one of mine and Jack's gigantic hand in the other. The squeeze sounds so cheese ball it makes me roll my eyes.

"Okay, squeeze it out. You're gonna be okay," Marco says with such calm in his voice. Then it happens. The simple act of another hand squeezing mine lightens my burden.

For the first time since Jen left me.

Chapter 14

They sure stretch the meaning of the word *lunch* here. All the sandwich choices come with a massive all-you-can-eat salad bar. Not a chip in sight. I'm sorry, but grief and health food are so not a match. I'm going to need to raid the vending machine and stockpile snacks to survive the next twenty-eight days in this hell. An entire bag of Sour Patch Kids, maybe a chaser of dark chocolate. Milk chocolate would be more for Jen.

I should probably find my group but I'm all talked out. I find a table in the back, opting to eat alone. I get a few bites in and realize it's futile. I have zero appetite. All I can think of is: Twenty. Eight. Days.

Our designated "crafting" area is actually an extra-long picnic table draped with a drop cloth and crammed with supplies. There's a canvas on a mini-easel for each one of us. Containers of tempera paint in every color under the rainbow and brushes of any size you could possibly want are in the center of the table within our reach. It's like preschool on steroids.

"Have a seat at the canvas with your name on it, then you can take the Post-it off. This afternoon we're going to address guilt."

"Oh, good." I sigh to Cass wryly. If Marco heard me, he ignores me.

"With grief and the loss of a loved one sometimes comes guilt about things that are out of our control. There's no shame attached to it. While you paint, we'll work through anything you might be grappling with."

"What does painting have to do with grief?" I ask.

"Sometimes it's easier to talk about hard things when you're doing something else," he answers. "This exercise isn't about how artistic you are. It's more about diverting your attention. You can paint whatever you like. While you do that, we'll talk."

Marco smiles, but my gut says they're loading us up with a fun activity so they can shoot us with reality.

Shifting around in my seat, I select a fan brush to make bigger strokes, figuring this will mask my glaring lack of talent. I decide on midnight blue and a beautiful violet as the colors to coat my canvas. Seated next to me, Graham reluctantly chooses a mop-like brush that's almost as thick as his hair. He dips it in crimson paint then takes a thinner brush to add baby-blue shading. Cass is way ahead of us. She's using an ultra-thin brush and several different colors, well on her way to outlining what looks like musical notes. Momentarily Ben hesitates, but with each stroke of his brush, it's clear he knows a little something about how to do this. His fluid movement and attention to detail on the faces stun me. He's a natural. Did not see that coming.

"When your loved one died, did you feel like there was something you could have done to prevent it? Was there something you wish you could have said? Let's talk about it," Marco encourages us.

Crap. I knew it. I've spent countless hours riddled with the guilt over what I might have been able to do to make a difference for Jen.

I swallow hard, eyes on my canvas, and I open my mouth voluntarily. "There hasn't been a day that's gone by since Jen took her life that I haven't felt that I could have done something. Should I have seen it coming? I mean, she was sitting next to me at dinner, then went home and killed herself. There had to have been a sign. And … I missed it."

I'm so grateful that Marco cuts in with a response.

He says, "Often when people commit suicide, no one sees it coming. People hide their depression because they don't think anyone will understand what they're going through."

"I don't know," I say, because I really don't. "I keep going back to the last time I saw her alive. We had spaghetti and meatballs with garlic bread, her favorite. She had two helpings. That should have tipped me off. She never had seconds on Sunday. Saturday, yes. Sunday, no. Like, never. She said Sunday seconds made you bloated Monday morning."

"Trust me, Kai. She was on a path that no one could have prevented. Suicide fills families with a whole lot of what-ifs," Marco adds.

I paint purple pillows under a dark blue sky as I listen to him and take it all in.

"You can't allow guilt to take over your life," Marco continues.

Graham drops his brush. "I should have been with Justin. Any other day, I would have been sitting in the car next to him."

"What purpose would that have served?" Marco questions him.

Graham shakes his head. "I wouldn't have to feel like this." He picks up his brush and turns his attention back to what looks like some kind of logo he's designing.

"I know exactly what you mean," Ben interrupts. "I was in the car with my parents and my little brother. Coming home from *my* science fair. Cory didn't even want to go but my parents made him. Now they're dead and he's fighting for his life. I got out of it with a few stitches. How can I not feel guilty?"

"The guilt that you all are expressing is very common in cases of suicide and being a survivor of a terrible accident. What's important to take away is that you are the sufferer, you did not cause the suffering," Marco says.

I like the sound of that, but I'm not sure I believe it. I focus on my colorful canvas.

Cass breaks the silence. "I was writing a song for my grandmother to surprise her for her birthday. I should have worked on it instead of going down to the shore with my friend Amy for the weekend. I was thinking of myself. Now she'll never hear it."

She points at the notes she's illustrated. "This is the melody I've been working on."

"Is that what you keep humming?" asks Ben.

Smiling, she nods.

Jack hasn't said anything. I'm not even sure he's been listening. He's razor focused on a camo-colored truck surrounded by pools of red.

Marco paces around, checking out each of our canvases. He wrinkles his nose at the sight of Jack's and moves behind Graham.

"What's that?" he asks.

"I woke up this morning replaying our last game in my head. This is Justin's lacrosse jersey with our school crest. He was so proud to be part of the team. He lit up whenever he put it on. We're the West Hills Academy Bears, our team colors are crimson and light blue."

I can tell he's moved at the sight of his brother's number, thirty-five. The thick black line through the three and the five is so graphic. So final.

My canvas is basically swirls of purple and blue with yellow stars and a crescent moon. Simple and clean. My take on Van Gogh's *Starry Night*.

I crane my neck toward Marco. "Jen's favorite color was purple. When I found her in her bed, she was surrounded by puffy purple pillows." I can't tear my eyes away from the canvas. "I hope that there really is a heaven and my sister is there and has found the peace she so desperately craved."

The familiar flood returns. Thankfully, Marco doesn't force me to keep sharing. Ben sees me tear up and takes the lead. "What do you think?" He tips his canvas in Marco's direction.

Ben's canvas looks like it could be a long-lost page from *Goodnight Moon* — another one that Jen loved to read to me. The painting shows four expertly crafted armchairs in bright colors. Seated in the chairs are a mom, a dad and two young boys. There's a kitten curled up next to a blazing fireplace. The windowsills covered in snowdrifts are to the right of the blazing fire. I want to be in that happy place right now.

"It's beautiful, Ben," I gush.

"It's what used to be." Suddenly the paint smears with his teardrops. It's all too much, if you want to know the truth. I move my brushes around nervously, Graham grinds his teeth and Cass snaps her gum.

Marco redirects himself to Jack. Taking in the canvas like the rest of us, Marco puts his hand on Jack's shoulder. It's hard to look at what he's painted: a Humvee, a bloodbath, not much more that's recognizable.

Jack says, "I have nightmares about my dad being ambushed with the gunfire and the explosions that must have followed. The senseless murder of my dad along with everyone in his platoon. No one made it out alive. Not one person. I hate the war but I loved my dad. I should have made that clear before he got on that plane. Every single day, I regret not telling him. When you said guilt, this is what I thought."

Marco shakes his head. "Everyone makes mistakes and has regrets. This is an opportunity to let yourself off the hook. Be kind to you. Nothing that happened was your fault. You could never have prevented any of these tragic events." I bet he's said this before, but we're all hearing it for the first time today.

The moment of silence isn't on purpose, it just happens. We're feeling. And thinking. Maybe Marco is right. "You can keep the paintings to remember to forgive yourselves," he says.

It's hard to be normal after that.

"You guys want to play Ping-Pong or something before dinner?" Jack finally asks, attempting a lighter note.

We all nod affirmatively except for Ben.

"I need to call my uncle. I want to check in on my brother. Maybe he woke up," he says, his voice so dog-tired.

Not giving it a second thought, I move toward him, circling my arms around his shoulders and hugging him hard. He slowly puts his arms around my waist and holds on like he never wants to let go. I feel his tears soak my shirt.

I don't care if we just met, this guy needs it.

Truth is that it feels pretty damn good to me, too.

Two birds. One stone.

Chapter 15

This cafeteria sure could use a face-lift, but the truth is that no one is here for the food or ambience. I wander over to check out the breakfast bar, hoping a *Top Chef* runner-up magically appeared overnight. Nope, that didn't happen. Still, I see pancakes and breakfast sandwiches, a slight improvement over yesterday's pasty oatmeal and limp bacon.

I turn away quickly and run right into Jack, in all his hotness.

"Last night was fun," he says, referring to the Ping-Pong extravaganza that raged on long after dinner.

"For you. Big winner," I tease. His toothy smile lights up his face.

"I'm competitive," he readily admits.

"I could tell when you nearly knocked the Ping-Pong ball down my throat in your quest for the match point in the last set."

"Sorry. No, I'm really not," he jokes, flashing a hundred-watt grin.

We each grab an egg sandwich to go. Hard to mess up eggs, sausage and cheese. I balance mine on my journal.

"Thanks to you, I didn't write in my journal last night. I was so drained I couldn't string together two sentences that were even semi-literate. I'm off to do it now."

"I went for a run at five thirty. Couldn't sleep." Then he pauses, watching me grab several packets.

"Ketchup? Really? On egg sandwiches?"

"If you haven't noticed, this place isn't known for their cuisine. Ketchup makes everything better. Trust me. My sister's refrigerator was stocked with every condiment you could imagine. Hot sauce, three different mustards. You name it, she had it and sometimes in duplicate."

"So, you're a lot like her?" he asks with such tenderness.

I blink back tears. "In some ways I guess I am."

"She must've been pretty kick-ass." There's no note of flirty, just kindness. He grabs a packet. "Okay, then. What the hell."

"You're gonna love it. Trust me."

He's iffy on the whole thing, I can tell by the way he's shaking his head.

"Okay, I'll give it a go. Later."

"Later. I'm gonna find a secluded spot lakeside for me and my journal."

"Good plan, see you at group," he says, heading off in the opposite direction.

Yeah, I watch his butt as he walks away. I mean, it's right there.

* * *

Leaning against the thick base of a majestic Fraser fir, I'm awestruck at the beauty before me. I look up to the morning sky, rays of sunshine peeking through the branches of the tree above the patch of ground I've claimed. A little patch of heaven.

"I hope you're okay, Jen," I say, hushed, to my sister, who doesn't answer back. But a squirrel crunches on an acorn nearby, giving me pause since it happens at the exact moment I look up. I'm not one to buy into the supernatural, but not gonna lie, this makes me wonder. TJ believes in reincarnation, and I wish I did, too. But that squirrel hasn't taken his beady little eyes off me. Jen would be thinking I've lost it. But maybe, just maybe … Highly unlikely my sister is now a squirrel but I like the gentle reminder that she's with me. That's what I'm going with since I need a crumb of anything to hang on to.

For a few hours last night, I forgot why I was here.

Then I woke up.

After a few bites of this Heinz-smothered sandwich, I rewrap it, open my journal and get down to jotting my thoughts. I did promise to try.

Sitting by the lake in the stillness of the morning, it's peaceful, so serene. I hope this is Jen's new normal. Sure isn't mine. It just seems so messed up if you really break it all down. Twenty-two years old. World traveler. Family that loves you. Good job. Kill yourself. It doesn't add up no matter how much I need it to.

That's the hardest part.

The guilt isn't so peaceful. It's so crushing at times I fear it will obliterate me completely. My brain is in a vise grip.

Tightening.

I just want to be me again. The Kai who loved life, who laughed at everything. That girl longs for normal. At least the *kind of normal my dysfunctional family had when Jen was part of it.*

Every day, I hope it gets better than the day before. So far, the act of a new friend giving me a Kleenex and sharing my ache is progress that I'll take.

* * *

Duke would love it up here, smells for days. Hiking up a trail near the lake, making my way to group, I take a deep breath of pine. I'd like to bottle this tranquillity to take with me. The reality of group has me desperate for some calm. The thing about the circle is that everybody participates even when they don't want to. I don't know if it actually makes it better or worse, but right now it only feels worse to me. I'm barely hanging on with Jen's suicide so when you pile on the weight of everyone else's feelings, it's almost too much.

But the suck is being spread around. Everyone is getting their fair share. I'm not alone and that helps. My mind wanders back to Dad's stash of scotch and Mom's bountiful supply of vodka. A little sip of either might help, since the Xanax are having no effect whatsoever, but that isn't happening so I drink in the natural beauty around me instead. It is kind of nice to be away from home for a moment. Away from everything. Today, it's enough.

"Hey," Graham says, walking toward me. "Didn't see you at breakfast."

He moves closer, hands in his pockets.

"Last night after the big Ping-Pong match I passed out before I could journal, so I took my breakfast to the lake and wrote. It was kinda chill."

"Really?"

I shrug. "Well, let's just say, I don't mind the writing part, I'm just not crazy about putting my feelings on paper, where anyone could read my truth. But I'm at a point where I need to try anything. You know?"

He kicks around the dirt. "Yeah, it's hard."

Before we can continue, the others join us. We all gravitate to the same spots we sat in yesterday. Jack is upbeat, smiling with his straight, pearly white teeth. I'm thinking he's purposely wearing tight T-shirts to taunt Cass and me. Truth be told, I think Cass is kind of into him. She was in full-tilt flirt mode during the Ping-Pong tournament last night, but I can't let myself go there. The last thing I need is a guy in the equation.

Sitting down next to Ben, I notice him scribbling in his journal.

"I don't really know what I'm doing with this. I'm more of a math and science guy," he admits.

"You're a killer artist, Ben."

His cheeks turn pink.

"It doesn't matter what you write as long as you're writing something," I say, mimicking Marco.

"Do you cry when you write in yours?" he asks so innocently. He's not like any of the guys I know. So innocent for a fifteen-year-old.

"Sometimes."

He fiddles with the silver chain he's never without. I notice some kind of medallion. I try not to stare but I fail.

"It's a St. Christopher medal. Patron saint of safe travels. My parents gave them to my brother and me when we were confirmed. I was wearing mine on the day of the accident. He wasn't."

Marco is a welcome sight after that. He's got a basket in one hand and a bottle of smartwater in the other.

"Morning, everyone." I suppose it's easy to be cheery when you're not forced to bare your soul to people you hardly know.

"He's got a basket. Christ," Graham says, all gloom and doom.

We greet him in unison, though we're not nearly as chipper. We're focused on the basket of terror.

Marco doesn't waste any time getting started. "Here's the plan. There are random questions folded in the basket. Each about an emotion associated with your loved one. All our group therapy sessions are designed to help you confront the tough things you're going through as well as happy memories."

I wouldn't mind a happy thought falling into my brain.

"When the basket makes its way around the circle, just reach in, pick a question. Answer it. If anyone else wants to make a remark about it, go for it. Then you'll pass the basket to the person on your right."

He moves gingerly around the outside of the circle to his spot, but hands the damn thing off to me on his way.

Reaching into the dark wicker basket is more than unnerving. Still, I do it. All eyes are on me. I'm the morning activity guinea pig. My shaky hand reaches in, drawing out a neatly folded piece of paper. I take my time unfolding it, nervous as all hell. Moving the paper from hand to hand. Fumbling until I open it and read it aloud.

No happy memory for me.

"'Anger is a common response to grief and loss. Give a recent example of such anger with the loss of your loved one.'" My voice drags as I read the piece of lined paper. May as well divulge my epic meltdown.

"I have a quilted headboard my sister and I made. She sent me postcards and quotes when she went to Europe for a year. I tacked each of them up there so I could see them every night before I went to sleep. They reminded me of her adventures and that she thought of me while she was there. I was so pissed off at her for killing herself that I tore them all down in a blind rage."

I take a measured breath and go on. "Then I cut off my hair. I was pretty drunk at the time. Completely out of control." God, I can't believe I just shared *that*.

"Why were you so angry?" Jack asks.

"Nothing in particular." Which is not really the truth.

I pause, then try again. "Everything."

"I get that," he says.

Graham shakes his head in agreement. "Your hair is badass."

I feel my face getting all hot and tingly. But not from rage.

"Are you angry *at* your sister?" Marco asks.

"No," I answer quickly. "You can't be angry at a dead person." Another lie.

"Can you?" Jack directs his question to Marco.

Marco explains. "Yes, it's actually quite common to be mad at someone for leaving you, more than you might think," he responds. "The important thing is to recognize it and let go of that and hang on to the love."

I'm done. I thrust the basket at Ben. He's hesitant at best as he reaches his hand in to draw out his question.

"It's a fill-in-the-blank. 'Before the death my biggest fear was …'" He stammers.

"Take your time, Ben," Marco reassures him.

"My biggest fear before my parents died was … I didn't really fear anything. They made me feel so safe. Today things are so much different. I fear, well, pretty much everything. I wake up every night with the same thoughts. I'm scared that my brother will die, I'm scared to be in a car on a freeway, I'm scared to be alone."

I see Jack press his hand on Ben's shoulder. "Every time I hear a car backfire or any loud noise, it scares the crap out of me. All I can think about is the sound my dad must have heard."

Incomprehensible.

"A big part of healing is to work through your fears until they no longer rule your life. Right now, that's easier said than done, I know. I get it. Communicating your feelings is a big part of it. Keeping them locked inside is toxic." Marco emphasizes this with such passion, I totally believe him.

Makes sense.

Still, not so easy.

Ben hands the basket to Jack. As he reads his note, the content demeanor disappears from his face along with the soft pink in his cheeks.

"'What was the most difficult thing for you to handle about the funeral?'"

That would be easy for me. I've got a top-ten list, at least. I flash back to the margarita machine, and getting hit on. Wonder what they'd think about that.

Not so easy for Jack. I cross my fingers and toes in hopes that Marco gives him a pass.

He doesn't. Jack wiggles around so much that I ache right along with him, but to his credit he presses on. "I never got to see him again, even dead. The bomb ..." His voice is muffled, trailing off into nowhere. We all cringe, knowing about roadside bombings from the nightly news.

Except not this close to home.

"I just can't go there right now." Cass was right. Jack's a hider.

"It's okay, Jack. Before we move on," Marco continues, "did any of you have an experience with something similar?"

I can't believe my lips engage. No hesitation. Just blabbering.

"Well, I got to see my sister and that didn't help. I found my sister in her apartment so I saw her dead right in front of me. Then I made my parents let me see her again before her funeral. It just wasn't sinking in that I would never lay eyes on her again once they closed her coffin. Even with that, I keep thinking she'll just show up. So far, no luck."

"Jack, do you think it would have mattered? You know, seeing an actual body?" Cass asks.

"I'll never know."

Jack bows his head to prevent us from seeing him cry even though it's impossible not to, and slides the basket to Graham, who's surrendered his brooding, bad-boy self and seems to be giving in to this like the rest of us. His expression now is more anxiety ridden, not like he's about to growl or bite.

He begins, "'Describe what it's like for you to visit the cemetery.'"

I straighten up, all my attention on Graham. I know a bit about this, too.

He swallows hard. "At first, I didn't want to go with my parents. Seeing them suffering made it harder for me. I felt like every time they looked at me, they saw him. So I started going by myself to talk to Justin like I used to do when he was alive. Only now he doesn't answer. No one knows I go as much as I do. Somehow sitting there with him helps me keep him close."

I think about lying next to Jen at the cemetery. "I feel like that when I visit my sister," I let slip out. Man, I can't stop talking.

"I haven't been to the cemetery since the funeral. I was in a daze that day. I'm just not prepared to see my parents' names together on some brass plaques on top of them," admits Ben.

Jack shifts around, shaking his head. "Me neither, Ben. I mean, there's nothing there but a headstone."

When I go to the cemetery, I see my sister. She's there under all that dirt. Inside a casket that keeps rain and bugs away. At least I have that. Who would ever have thought I'd be saying I'm grateful for that?

But I am.

Cass reaches into the basket as Graham passes it her way.

"'If you could say one more thing to your loved one, what would it be?'" she reads.

Cass, usually so poised, loses it. "I would thank her. I don't think I ever really thanked her for saving my siblings and me when my mother picked getting high over us. I hope she knew." I suspect this breakdown was a long time coming. Jack hands her the box of tissues.

I wrap her pinkie in mine.

There's a cloud of heartache hovering over us this morning. Marco surveys all of us before standing.

"I think we'll take a break for now. This afternoon we're going kayaking."

I am ridiculously relieved to know there will be no sharing, just a little paddling. Perfect. Something light is exactly what the doctor of death ordered. We all stand, clasping our hands without being told. It just kind of happens, all our fingers just fall into place, hanging on to hope.

Chapter 16

Kayaking. I'm okay with this. No thinking, just doing. All the "feels" are getting to me and we're only a few days in. At orientation they stressed the importance of exercising. Alison stood up in front of all the parents and kids and told everyone, "Physical activity will help release negative energy."

I'm all for that but not so sure I can pull it off. My negative energy is infinitely greater than my positive. And it's been a while since I've exerted anything other than my heart.

Some things are the same, wherever you are. I still feel lost. For now, I just have to worry about a little exercise. I can do that.

"What are you wearing?" I ask Cass.

"A bikini with some shorts, I guess." She holds up a leopard-print bikini the size of a postage stamp and some cut-off jean shorts. "You?"

"Board shorts and a bikini top." I show her my black Hurley board shorts with bright green piping and a matching green halter top.

Cass disappears into the bathroom to change, hollering out as she goes, "Can I admit something to you?"

"Sure!" I yell back.

She pops her head out. "I hope Jack and Graham don't wear shirts."

Thinking about that puts a smirk on my face and fills my head with all kinds of wrong. As I'm contemplating that, a familiar wave of guilt washes over me. Cass runs gel through her hair as she pops out of the bathroom, checks the mirror. I scour my drawer for a T-shirt to wear. I see a navy tank top with a smiley emoji wearing sunglasses. TJ tucked it in my Christmas stocking last year.

Score.

Just what I needed.

"How can I be thinking about guys when my sister is gone? What kind of person does that?" I ask.

"A person who isn't dead. You're sixteen and allowed."

It's not that I don't believe Cass but I secretly hope Marco touches on this. I could use a little validation from the expert here.

I shrug at her. "Let's go or we'll be late."

On our way to the lake, we pass by a picnic table of kids who look about six or so covered in paint and glitter. Alison, their leader for the day, waves at us.

"Hey."

We stop and admire their arts-and-crafts projects.

"What are they doing?" I ask.

"Making grief masks. Expressing their feelings with art."

It always circles back to *that*. All the raw feelings.

"We're on our way to kayak," Cass offers, though Alison didn't ask. We make our way down the path through the enormous trees to our group meet-up.

"I wouldn't mind one of those masks to hide behind." I surprise myself by uttering those words out loud.

"It's hard to imagine how tough it is for them. I know how much this stinks and we've got about ten years on them," she remarks.

I think about that for a minute.

"Some of them lost their parents like Ben and Jack. And others have parents who lost a child, one of their siblings, like Graham and me. Maybe a grandparent."

Yeah, that would suck.

"How are your parents dealing with it?" Cass wonders aloud.

"Oh man," I say. "I could write a book. Some days it's like nothing ever happened. We never talk about it. My dad is back to work at his law office, my mom is brokering houses. I just spiraled out of control with no one noticing until I cut my hair off."

"That must have been so hard," she says, touching my forearm as we get to our afternoon destination. I am so grateful I could cry, but I try to be cool.

"Cass, thanks for … just hanging out."

The first thing that strikes me at the lake is that there are only three kayaks: one a dark blue, one fire-engine red and a pastel yellow one resting on the bank. Each one is built to hold two people.

"We're gonna be paired up," I whisper to Cass.

"Please let me be stuck with Jack." She cackles so loudly, I elbow her in the side.

"I hope you are, too."

Passing the kayaks on our way to the lake's edge, I take off my Nikes and toss them aside to test the water. It's cool, refreshing as it snakes through my toes. The pebbles underfoot are smooth, massaging my feet with each step I take. This is infinitely better than group.

Then I sense that I have company and turn quickly to see Graham standing a few inches from my face.

"Hey, thanks for the Kleenex. Wanted to tell you earlier but I'm not much of a talker and that morning wore me out. That was kind of embarrassing. You know?" he says with a lopsided grin. His upper incisor is a little bit crooked.

"Nothing to be embarrassed about. It was honest," I reassure him.

"The crying thing is totally new for me, especially in front of people. Like, I've never done it. Until Justin." He's as hot as Jack in his own way, I decide.

Even with the sun beating down on us, Graham has that beanie on. He's not even sweating. How's that possible? I already feel a little damp under my armpits and I'm so not the girl who sweats.

Like the Xanax being zapped, the timing of this couldn't be worse.

Marco calls out to us, breaking the mood. "Everyone, over here."

The five of us comply. I edge close to Jack, who's filling out his knee-length pin-striped board shorts and dark green tank top. The green brings out the hazel of his eyes and accentuates his close-cut blond hair rather nicely. He's Jen's type, for sure. She had a weak spot for green eyes and bulging muscles.

"You're onto something with the ketchup," Jack coughs up, bringing a grin to my face. I knew it. Ketchup makes everything better.

Marco gives us the lowdown. "We're going to explore the other side of the lake. Graham, you're with Kai. Jack, you and Cass will be together. Ben, buddy, it's you and me."

We amble toward one another, pairing up per our instructions, dragging kayaks through the pine needles and over the rocks, ultimately landing them in the water. I give Cass a thumbs-up when no one is looking. In one swift move, Jack removes his tank with a swooping motion. By the OMG look beaming across Cass's face, I'm guessing that caused a mini-earthquake in her stomach. I'm not gonna lie, I get it. His washboard abs are not hard to look at.

Even at grief camp.

Sweating quickly becomes a problem of the past as I move waist-deep into the water across from Graham, who's guiding our vessel. The chilly water's giving me goose bumps. Unless it's something else.

Graham steadies the kayak. "Hop in, I'll hold it still, I got you," he reassures me, grinning as the sun hits him just so. The crooked tooth sure adds some character to his face. I find myself returning the smile before I realize what I've done.

Hoping I don't tip the kayak, I propel myself out of the water and onto the top of it, landing safe and sound on my first attempt.

"Move up to the front, you're smaller than me," he suggests. I hear a splash next to us. Jack and Cass dumped their kayak over, sending them both tumbling into the lake, and ripples of water are coming our way. They resurface consumed by laughter and lightness. This could be good.

Graham masters the vault into the kayak and scoots up behind me, placing each of his legs next to each of mine, straddling me. The coarse dark hair on his legs rubs against my thighs as he shifts into place.

These goose bumps are definitely not from the chilly lake water. Last time I felt these was sophomore year. "Right side first. You okay?" he asks, handing me a paddle.

Kim Turrisi

"Yeah. I'm good." Back to lying. I'm not sure what I am.

"You know you light up when you talk about your sister? Something in your eyes, even when you're talking about the hard stuff. I wish I could have met her," he says with his first smooth stroke through the still water. I do the same in unison. Instinctively, I turn my head halfway to answer him.

"She was pretty amazing. That's the hardest part. It came out of nowhere. One minute she was there, the next gone. Forever. I know you get it."

"I'll never forget my mom's scream when we got the phone call. I knew something horrible had happened. I felt it right before the call. I don't know how to explain it. They say it's a twin thing."

"I've heard that."

"It's totally true."

Out on the water, away from everyone, Graham is so much more at ease, his shoulders relaxed. Jen used to say water calms everyone down. "It feels good to be out here, like it's any old afternoon," he notes, laughing.

"Yeah, that. I have to admit, it makes me miss the beach. And my friends. Beach parties are a big part of my summer. I'm not really a camp girl."

"There's a sandpit near the rec room. We could hang out there sometime. That would be kinda like the beach," he tries.

"It's a stretch but I'm game." Liking the new light Kai.

Gliding through the water, not a care in the world. I'll take it even if it's just for a few minutes. Graham leans up, almost touching his chin to my shoulder.

"How mad were your parents about your hair?" He stifles a laugh.

159

I think about my dad freaking out.

"My parents can be a little uptight, so having a daughter shear her hair in a pill-popping rage did not sit well," I admit.

"My parents aren't uptight and they would flip out if I just chopped my hair off. Justin wanted to shave his head for lacrosse and my mom lost her shit."

We keep our strokes cutting through the water in perfect sync. Maybe it's easier to talk freely because we share something so huge. Whatever it is, the gnawing in my stomach is slowly dissipating.

"You said you had a golden retriever. It's my favorite breed. We had one growing up. Rocco. Had him since we were two. We lost him last year. He was a great dog."

"I'm so sorry. Duke was Jen's dog but now he's mine. I miss him so much." I can't even go there. "So ... did Rocco hog the bed? Duke is a total bed hog." If Jen could hear this conversation, she would be so teasing me about using her dog to flirt with a guy.

Yes, I am flirting at grief camp.

"Totally!"

"Think you'll get another dog?" I ask.

He slows the kayak down using the paddle.

"We were going to rescue one after the season ended. But now I don't even want to get a dog. It's like I don't know how to be without Justin. We shared a room, friends and sports. Now it's just me. Alone." A twinge of sadness creeps into his cracking voice. He clears his throat.

Just me echoes in my head.

Alone is brutal.

Alone is lonely.

Alone is final.

"At least it wasn't his choice. That's the absolute worst part for me."

The paddling stops momentarily.

Graham is quiet until he's not. "The worst for me is when I'm on the lacrosse field. Justin and I have been teammates since we started playing T-ball. When we had to choose a sport, it was hands-down lacrosse. He really lit up on the field. He loved the game. He owned it. Everything about it reminds me of Justin now. You know?"

We maneuver the kayak through the calm waters to catch up to the others. It's so serene. Death nowhere in sight, just life.

I take a moment to answer him. "I do. I was with my mom at the grocery store a few days after Jen died. She stopped to pick up something to grill for dinner. Chicken, I think. Maybe steak. Doesn't really matter. All I wanted were some Sour Patch Kids and Red Vines. Turns out that the candy shares an aisle with greeting cards. I rounded the corner and ran right into a slew of 'Happy Birthday, Sister' cards. I burst into hysterics right there in the middle of aisle eight. My mom had to practically carry me out of the store. I was mortified. But you never know when you'll be ... reminded."

"Yeah." He doesn't need to say anything else. He knows.

Marco points his paddle to a secluded area where a bank sticks out into the lake.

"How about we head over there and take a break?"

My arms are like noodles. I'm not used to such a strenuous arm workout. Any workout, in fact. But Graham certainly is. Sneaking a look back I see that every muscle in his arm moves to the beat of each stroke with no sign of letting up or wanting to. I get back to our conversation. "Clearly Marco's ploy worked. I haven't talked about my sister to anyone like this. It's actually pretty easy," I say.

"He knows what he's doing. I feel bad for being such an asshole to him when I got here."

"Thinking you weren't the first."

"I gotta find a way to fix that," he says.

"You will."

We sit there like that for a minute, just floating, until suddenly Graham starts to rock our kayak and capsizes it, tossing both of us into the water. I screech just a little bit right before I go under. When I surface, I splash water in his face. We start a mini water war, seeing who can get who to back down first. I'm not giving up.

When I don't relent, he swims up behind me and dunks me under with both hands.

"First round goes to me," he shouts, throwing his arms up in the air, the victor.

I laugh it off, relaxing my body, treading water.

Cass cackles as she jumps out of her kayak and swims toward us, leaving Jack solo, laughing his ass off. I swim next to his kayak.

"You think it's funny?" I taunt him. And in one swift motion, I grab the hull and flip him over, too.

"Yes!" I scream, bopping up and down in the lake. Jack dives under, heading toward Marco and Ben.

"Jump, Ben!" Knowing they're next in line for dunking, they join us before being forced into the water. We all take it easy on Ben; he seems a tad more frail than the rest of us. Almost his entire family gone in an instant. And his brother ... jeez.

Goofing around in the water like teenagers without a care in the world as the sun ducks behind the massive trees is better than any pill. I haven't felt like this since ... I can't even remember.

"It's after three, we better head back," Marco says.

Two hours. Not a single tear. But when I remember that, I remember Jen. And just like that, I'm swallowed by sadness again. My spirits drop like a bomb. I wipe the smile from my face and haul myself back into the kayak for the paddle back to camp.

If Graham notices my about-face, he keeps it to himself.

* * *

Freshly showered after our afternoon outing, Cass straightens up her bed, tucking her bottom sheet under the box spring, totally reminding me of my mom. I notice her grab something from under her pillow and hold it to her nose.

"It was my grandmother's sachet." She mists up. "Rose petals and rosemary. She made them for everyone in her Bunco group. I found it in her housecoat when I was boxing up her things. I wanted to take a piece of her with me."

She slips it back under her pillow.

"I'm going to the rec hall to hang out, maybe watch a movie or something. You want to come?" Cass asks.

"No thanks, I'm gonna call my parents then lose myself in a book. I'm not up for being around a crowd."

"Got it. Right now, I just need noise to fill my brain, so it works out for both of us."

Secretly, I'm thrilled for some time alone. My personal space, my sister, all of it.

I shoot a text to Emily and TJ.

Hey, I'm still alive. It's not awful. Miss you guys. Xo K

I tap my Facetime and call my mom.

Her face pops onto my phone. She's at the kitchen counter. "Hi, sweetie."

"Hey, Mom." I greet her louder than I wanted to. I'm really glad to see her face and her earrings. I hear Duke barking in the background.

"Hi, buddy!" I yell.

Mom waves the phone in front of his golden snout.

"Are you being a good boy, Dukey?"

More barking. I think he is.

"I miss you, bud." I manage to get that in just before Mom hijacks the screen.

"Great to see you, Kai. How are you, honey?"

"Hanging in there. Group therapy fills me with anxiety but I really am trying. Harder than I've ever tried to do anything in my life. A lot of the stuff we talk about is so personal. I just relive Jen's death over and over but it seems to make sense. As much sense as this can possibly make. You know what I mean? How are you guys?"

"We went to our first therapy session." She tugs on her earring. Just picturing my mom and dad sitting together with a therapist makes me squirm.

"How was that?"

"Not so great. They say the first time is the hardest."

The corners of her eyes begin to leak. "I've picked up the phone about a dozen times to call her."

"I've actually called her cell phone just to hear her greeting," I confess.

"Doesn't that make closure that much more impossible?" she asks.

"I'm not sure I'll ever get closure." Probably not what she wants to hear from grief camp, but whatever.

"Your dad and I are going to South Seas for a long weekend," she tells me.

Are you effing kidding me, a vacation? I almost scream. But I control myself.

"I think that's amazing, Mom. Good for you guys." I try to sound neutral. Not judgey.

"I'm so proud of you for sticking with camp, Kai."

That brings all the happy. "Thanks. I better get going; I have homework, if you can believe it. We have to write about our feelings every day. It's not so easy but it's part of it."

"Maybe I should do that."

That admission surprises me.

"You should!" Then I don't know how to go on. "I just wanted to check in and let you guys know I was thinking about you."

"We've been hoping to hear from you. We don't want to push you. We love you, Kai, don't ever forget that."

"You, too."

I hang up and find two texts waiting for me.

Saw your parents yesterday, we went over for dinner. Duke misses you. LOL. So do I. xo Em

Miss you madly. Going to Em's to watch a Teen Mom marathon. xo TJ

Turning my iPad on, I go right to my iTunes library and highlight a playlist Jen put together for me a few months ago. All obscure bands she discovered while traveling. I chill to the beat, thinking about all that my sister gave me in such a short time. I remember one day at the beach, when we were listening to a haunting My Morning Jacket song — "Wonderful," I think — she grabbed my hand and got all serious, and was like, "Music is the gateway to your soul." I had no idea what the hell she was talking about at the time. I do now. Grabbing a throw pillow, I plop down with my journal.

Today felt almost like a typical day until I remembered Jen is still dead and always will be. I talked about it a little bit with Graham. Out of the comfort zone for me but he made it easy. Mostly. This place isn't as bad as I anticipated. In a peculiar way it's almost nice to be surrounded by people in the same place that I am (emotionally). Emily and TJ are there for me but have no idea what it's like to have their world shatter, and everyone here does. Strength in numbers.

I trade my journal in for *Franny and Zooey*. When I pick the book up, a strip of four pictures falls out on my lap. I'd tucked it there before I left and forgot all about it. In my hand, I hold us. Four pictures of me and my sister in the photo booth at an engagement party for one of Dad's partners' sons just a few short weeks before her death. I scrutinize each pixel, hunting for any detail I might have missed.

Nothing.

Her putting bunny ears behind my head in one. Both of us giving peace signs in another. Blown-out cheeks and crossed eyes in a third. Lastly, me cracking up while she tickled me. Her eyes twinkling in every single shot.

Absolutely no indication that soon she would choose to be gone for good.

I wish I could talk to her. Maybe she could slip me a clue, tell me it will all be okay.

On the verge of breaking down, I reach for my cell phone and dial the only number I have ever committed to memory. I listen, staring at the carefree face in the pictures in front of me with no answers.

My sister's cheery voice greets me: "It's Jen. You know what to do." I listen to it another six times. The answer is still the same.

No, I don't.

Chapter 17

After a harrowing morning exercise of sharing, sharing and more sharing, we retreat. My group and I choose to hang in the way-back corner of the dining hall long after the others have gone. Together saying nothing. There's peacefulness in the quiet.

I'm trying to let go of the special-treat fail at lunch. They made a huge deal about giving us french fries, but they were so soggy they bent in half when you dipped them in ketchup. *That* should be against the law.

I miss TJ and Emily but these four are really growing on me. Cass takes a bag of chips from her backpack and slides it across the table to me.

A bag of chips.

"I know the french fries were a bust," she says. So thoughtful.

Jack sees. "They really were. How about sharing?"

I tear open the bag and offer it to *my group*. I like the way that sounds. I like the way this feels.

"I'm going up to the rec hall to Skype with my sister," Cass drops casually as she pushes her chair back to stand.

My neck snaps in her direction and I fight the urge to say, *Are you fucking kidding me?* She couldn't keep that to herself?

It's like rubbing salt into an open wound. I fight to swallow the bitterness and heavy heart that one word brings.

"Jesus Christ" just tumbles out of my mouth, resentment filling me.

All eyes shift to Cass, who can't help but feel the sting.

"Oh, Kai. I'm so sorry," she swiftly apologizes.

She starts to reach for me but wisely rethinks that. Instead, she picks up her plate to leave. She can't get outta my face soon enough for my liking.

"I wasn't thinking."

I don't want to be an asshole about one word but it's just so loaded. "Obviously."

As soon as Cass dashes away, Graham is the first to try to deal with it. "That so sucked. I'm sorry, Kai. You were totally cool about it. I think if anyone besides Ben said they were going to see their brother, I'd flip out."

I try to be reasonable. "Thanks. I guess I'm gonna have to get used to hearing stuff like that though. So are you, right?" Even as I say it, I don't think I will ever get used to it. Could we take the word out of the English language?

He shakes his head. Jack breaks the silence. "Anyone want to go for a hike or run before group? Might help."

"Sure, why not?" Graham answers.

Me? "Pass. Maybe I'll go to the lake. See you later." I'm too raw to be with them right now.

Ben gets up. "I barely slept last night so I think I'll just go back to the cabin to take a nap."

Jack bro-knuckles him but Ben misses, catching nothing but air. Before Ben can even react, Jack quickly grabs his arm like he meant to, saving Ben from embarrassment.

"Later, dude."

I catch Jack's eye. Damn, that was a really sweet gesture. He cocks his head and half winks at me.

Down at the lake, I try something new: meditation with the help of music on my iPod. Call me old-school, but I like my phone and my music separate, plus the iPod was a gift from Jen a couple of years ago to celebrate my starting high school. I downloaded some New Age music for meditation after that whole Janie thing went down at school. Emily made me do it. Confession: I so did not want to. But picturing Cass chatting it up with her sister when I can't talk to mine sends me spiraling. I need something to bring me back, and maybe this is it.

A flock of birds crisscrosses the lake, dodging back and forth. Ducks swim in circles before me. The way they are perfectly spaced out reminds me of Jen's handwriting.

Before the last letter.

Reminders are everywhere.

Around every corner.

At any moment, a simple word or memory can derail me.

I wonder how long it will take for them to stop turning up, threatening to swallow me whole. They say time heals all wounds. If that's true, will I forget Jen? I don't want that.

Ever.

Closing my eyes, I let the soothing sounds of waves roll through my earbuds.

I should have done this a few weeks ago. So chill. Really lost in no thoughts.

I half open one eye, checking my watch. Yeah, about forty-five seconds have flown by. This is not happening.

Clearing my mind before our afternoon group proves futile. I can't switch my brain to the off position even for a few brief moments. Not even with waves. An aroma of sandalwood with a hint of cedar fills my nose. I'm pleasantly surprised to find I have company, and for once he isn't wearing his signature beanie.

"Hey, I don't want to bug you," he says. I squint my eyes to see Graham, his jet-black hair unruly and damp.

"It's all good. You saved me from a meditation fail. I'm not very good at quieting my head."

"Me neither."

"How was the run?"

"Didn't really help." He laughs at himself. "But hanging with Jack was all right. What he did with Ben was pretty cool."

"It got me, too," I readily admit.

He rests on the pine-needle cushion next to me, managing to avoid the pinecones.

"Lose your beanie?" I tease.

He avoids my eyes. "I haven't taken it off much since Justin died, other than to shower or swim. It was his."

What a shitbag thing to say when this guy is being nothing but nice to me. If I could kick myself, I would.

"Oh, I'm really sorry, Graham."

"How would you know? I know it's stupid but it's like when I have it on, he's with me."

"Not at all. I still sleep in my sister's shirt. I'm afraid to wash it. If I do, her smell will disappear with the rest of her."

As he taps his feet on the ground nervously, his untied laces click on the sides of his work boots.

"I understand. Justin and I shared a room even after our parents bought a house with four bedrooms. We hung out all the time and it just didn't seem right, being down the hall, you know? His side of the room smells like his collection of AXE body spray. It used to bug the shit out of me. Now the smell just brings me back."

"Is that what you're wearing?"

"It's called Black Chill. I even brought him out here."

He's really cute when he laughs at himself.

"I like it."

I feel my cheeks heat. Is what's happening what I think is happening? My stomach feels all tickly.

He reaches over, covering my soft hand with his callused one. "Is this okay?"

I let him know the answer by wrapping my fingers one by one in his. He catches me stealing a glance at him and I don't bother turning away. I like what's looking back at me. His touch reminds me that I'm very much alive.

Exchanging a half smile, we sit in silence near the wide-open stillness of the lake until I break away. It's like a perfect storm of wonder is happening.

* * *

Strolling up together for group, Graham and I cause an eyebrow or two to raise among our teeny Tree House family even though we've long since dropped our clasped hands. I make a point of waiting until he sits down in the circle so I can find a spot elsewhere.

"Today we're going to tackle the day your loved one died. You'll each talk about your experience with that. Feel free to join in the conversation even if it isn't your turn," Marco explains. "Who wants to start?"

No brainer. Anyone but me.

"I'll go," Jack pipes up first.

"I was eating a bowl of Cap'n Crunch. My mom was glued to CNN because the night before they reported a bombing of a village close to where my dad was stationed. We'd been down this road before so I figured it was another false alarm. Until the doorbell rang. I didn't have to look outside to know there were two officers in dark blue full-dress uniforms on the other side of the front door. I sat alone in the living room and listened as they broke the news to my mom: 'We regret to inform you that your husband died in a battle that killed his entire platoon,' then went on and on with their canned speech about how sorry they were for our loss and how proud we should be that he died protecting our country."

"That must have been so tough to hear," Cass says.

Tough to hear like the word *sister*. I have to admit it still stings. I try to shake it off. Nope, the mad still sticks.

"The worst part about it is that he was on his last tour. Only nine more months and he would have been home free. Back with us for good. A war I don't fucking agree with and it took my dad away from us. It's bullshit," Jack rages. "And I'll never get to say goodbye." His voice is overcome with raw emotion.

I can totally relate.

"Never getting to say goodbye is excruciating. One of the hardest things to get a grip on when you lose someone you love," Marco tells us.

Jack looks spent. Cass clears her throat and takes a run at the topic.

"My grandma had a really aggressive cancer, so it's not like we didn't know there was a possibility that she would lose her battle. We just weren't ready. I guess you're never really ready to lose a loved one."

A round of head bobs from everyone to her. And my anger disappears listening to her. She's not the enemy. She's an ally.

"She was in the middle of her chemo treatments and her heart just gave out. The chemo that was supposed to save her became too much for her body to handle. It wasn't even the freakin' cancer that killed her. How ironic is that? The day she died, my mother came to school to pick us up in her crappy car. That could only mean something disastrous had happened. She never does that, it was always my grandmother."

She looks around the circle, face wrapped in sadness. "My grandma was more of a mother to me than my mom will ever be."

The open wounds just fester. Jen was more of a mom to me than my own mother, too. I wipe the back of my hand across my eyes.

Ben opens up without being prodded. "I was asleep in the backseat of my parents' car with my brother. The noise when the cars collided … all that metal slamming together, ripping through our car."

It's like he's in a trance as he recounts the horror of that fateful night, shaken to his core.

"Then it got so quiet, eerily still. It was so puzzling after all that commotion. Next thing I remember was hearing cries next to me. It was Cory, until he went silent. Minutes later, more noise. Sirens. And the screaming. So much screaming from everywhere. My dad was gone before the paramedics got there. When they got my mom out on the gurney, they started CPR. But it was too late for her, too. I stood helplessly next to the stretcher while a paramedic straddled her, pushing on her chest over and over, then watched her take her last breath. After that, it just gets fuzzy."

"Oh, man. Ben ..." Graham manages.

"I wake up to that sound almost every night. It torments me."

As Ben is speaking, I close my eyes and see my sister in that coffin. I'm looking at her but she's not looking at me. That's what I wake up to.

His eyes plead with me to take my turn.

I bite my lower lip, drawing blood. "The day my sister died was just an ordinary Tuesday. My best friend, TJ, and I were trying to decide what to wear to our high school prom, which I didn't even care about. I was going to write an English paper, then we were going to hit up Taco Tuesday. That was the plan until my world collapsed. So much can happen in a single moment ... I never realized that."

My voice is shaky. I'm no longer answering the question but I can't stop talking and no one stops me. "I picked up the mail after school like always. Except on this day there were three handwritten letters waiting, one for each of us, from Jen. I should have known that wasn't a good sign. No one sends you a letter anymore, especially if they only live a few miles away. Anyway, that's how I found out she was dead. It was all in the letter. Life got to be too much for her. That's what it said. I raced to her apartment to save her but it was too late, she was already gone."

I visualize Jen sprawled on her bed like she's taking a nap. "My dad checked out. My mom was fixated on making my sister's death an event. I mean, she had a DVD of Jen's life in pictures playing on a loop at the reception right after we buried her. I thought one of us was going insane."

I don't bother trying to stop the surge of tears. It's useless.

"The three of us went to our separate corners of the house. I numbed the pain with as much booze as I could drink until I couldn't cope any longer and I lost my grip completely."

I don't have to look back to see whose hand is gently rubbing my back. He doesn't budge. Kneeling next to me, he begins to share his story.

"I was in my room studying for an American History test. My dad was watching ESPN while he finished up a PowerPoint presentation for a big meeting. I heard the phone ring. It was 10:42 p.m. I felt a twinge right before the phone rang. Something felt off, you know that gut feeling? Late-night calls only mean one thing. Bad news. My mother's scream confirmed it. I knew Justin was dead. I feel that same pang at 10:42 every night."

I feel his pain so hard that our arms naturally gravitate around each other. No one blinks. We're two only children bound by solitude. Graham and I cling to each other like we are on a lifeboat that's about to go under. I hear the others in the group sniffling but I can't seem to let go of the back of Graham's striped T-shirt. We linger, then separate hesitantly, gathering ourselves for the ceremonial end of our group therapy.

We end the session with the ritual squeeze that I've come to crave. It's like the five of us against the world.

With a private island reserved for just Graham and me.

Chapter 18

With all of the days running together loaded with feelings, I need a break. As I'm wandering around camp, clearing my head before lunch, the screams of the younger kids break into my Zen (or what little I've been able to scare up after the morning group activity, which was like Scrabble but we were supposed to spell out descriptions of our grief). When I get a little closer, I notice that Alison is juggling paints and the group of kids are running amok.

"Need some help?" I offer. I could use a break from myself.

She looks like she might cry. "*Yes!* Can you help me wrangle them up to the table to get them started with this activity?"

"Sure," I say. Rounding up most of the kids is actually a much-needed bright spot. Kids love when you chase them, and the unabashed joy in their tiny squeals melts me. I was one of those kids. I made Jen chase me at the beach, not a care in the world. I'm sure she could have caught me easily but she never did. She'd let me run and run until she picked me up and twirled me around and around until I laughed so hard, I cried. As Alison corrals the supplies to get them started, I help her get the kids hunkered down for their activity.

All the kids but one.

I notice one little boy sitting off by himself next to a tree, digging a hole with the heel of his tennis shoe, kicking dirt in the air. I cruise over to his spot, squatting down next to him. "Hey, buddy, wanna join the paint party?"

Nothing. He studies the sock he's moving up and down his skinny leg.

"My name is Kai, what's yours?" I gently nudge him to talk.

"Aaron," his tiny voice pipes up.

"I could really use a friend to partner up with. I was thinking maybe you'd like to work with me." I reach out for his hand. His head tilts up. I meet his heavy eyes with a smile. There's no return smile but he does secure his itty-bitty fingers around mine.

Taking his hand, I coax him over to the table. We sit at the end, away from the noise of the other kids, in front of a small canvas and small tins of color. I hand him a brush to persuade him to join in.

Still gripping my hand, his voice splintering, he says, "I don't want to paint anything about my mom today." *Boy, can I relate to you,* I think to myself. Instinctively, I reach around him and stroke his back as I continue our conversation.

"You don't have to. You know what I would love?"

Aaron shakes his head side to side.

"I have a dog at home named Duke. He's a golden retriever, and I really miss him. Maybe you could paint me a picture of him to hang in my cabin. I would really like that."

He slips his hand from mine to pick up a brush. I catch Alison observing it all unfold from the opposite end of the table. He perks up with each stroke of the brush.

"I have a dog, too. My mom got him for me when I turned six last year, before she got sick."

He moves the brush on the canvas while he chatters on.

"His name is Corduroy."

"Like the bear?"

"It's my favorite book. Mommy used to read it to me every night."

"I loved that book when I was your age, too."

So much in common with a six-year-old.

"She's in heaven now. Daddy says it's better because she's dancing in fields of flowers. The cancer doesn't hurt anymore."

I struggle to hold back tears. "That's a good thing, Aaron."

"I miss her," he says quietly.

"I bet she misses you, too." He leans close, tucking his head under my arm, and we stay there until my arm practically goes numb.

Then Alison ambles over, bending toward him. "Aaron, why don't you get in line with everyone else? Melia is taking all of you to have lunch. It's peanut butter and jelly, your favorite."

He wriggles out of his seat, ever so slightly cheered up, proudly handing me the canvas of Duke before he goes. It's a mishmash free-form picture with a stick-figure dog in the center, and I couldn't love it more.

I ruffle his hair. "It's beautiful, Aaron. You made my day."

Alison speaks when he's halfway to the dining hall. "You were really terrific with him, Kai. I can't thank you enough. Sometimes we don't have enough hands to go around, especially when one of the young ones needs a little extra attention."

"I think he helped me more than I helped him," I freely admit.

Now I understand why Jen did all the volunteering. It gave her something nothing else could. An undeniable sense of purpose. Yet, even that wasn't enough for her. It's enough for me.

She squeezes reassurance into my arm. "Come back anytime."

They're big on the squeeze thing here. I'm a fan.

* * *

Cass opens the door of our cabin just as I'm balancing Aaron's masterpiece against the wall. Things have been icy between us though I'm easing off. I mean, I know she didn't mean to rub it in my face that she has a sister and I don't ... anymore.

"Where did you disappear to after group?" she attempts.

"Went for a hike," I short-answer her.

Cass tugs on the back of my shirt. "Can we talk?"

I mellow out. She is my roommate. I'm not an asshole. I'm just broken.

"It's fine. Really."

She turns me around so we're face-to-face. "Kai, I would never say or do anything to hurt you. It was insensitive of me."

"I know. I'm sorry I've been so distant. I can't lose anyone else. Can we just put it behind us?"

She reaches for me. "Deal. And for the record, I'm not going anywhere."

"So my hike. I ended up hanging out with Alison and her group of kids. She has the seven and unders."

She points to the painting, joking with me. "Is that what you did?"

"I met the sweetest little boy who just lost his mom. Only six. He drew it for me. It's my dog." I crack up.

"His mom. God," Cass says.

Which makes me think of my own mom for a second. I promise I could make an argument for my pain being greater than anyone else's. But is it worse than my mom's? How do you even measure that? I take a photo of the painting to text to Mom.

Having a good day. Hope you guys are, too.

I even add a few purple heart emojis before I send it.

* * *

When Cass and I are making the trek up the hill toward the dining hall, we hear Jack yell to us from a clearing in the woods: "Over here!" We both do a double take when we see that the guys have lunch set up for us. All three of them, even Ben, who is beaming from ear to ear.

"We thought we'd change things up and eat outside, do something different. What do you think?" Graham asks.

I take it all in. "I think you guys are pretty sweet." I can't believe that just fell out of my mouth. Saying something like that to a group of guys is like speaking a foreign language. Grief camp is turning me upside down.

There are sandwiches, bags of chips and sodas sitting on an oversize plaid blanket. The guys are all lounging around it.

"No guy has ever planned a picnic for me before," Cass discloses.

Ben chimes in. "Now three of them have."

We all eat sandwiches, cross-legged.

"That was a rough morning," Graham recalls.

"The worst yet," Ben says. There goes his smile. That's the way it is here at grief camp. One minute you're fine, and the next you have a memory that's been jogged by the littlest thing and you're tumbling back down the rabbit hole.

"These ups and downs are rough," I throw in before I open my chips.

"But now at least there are some ups. Don't you feel better talking about it?" Cass asks, ever the beacon of positivity.

"All the talking hurts," Ben remarks. He pushes his food to the side. There's that yo-yo thing again. The ups and downs of it all just swallowed Ben.

Cass checks her phone. "I'm gonna take the rest of my food up to the cabin if it's okay with you guys. I just had a thought about the song I've been working on so I need to get a jump on it."

"You're bailing after we cooked for you? That hurts," Jack says, clutching his heart and acting all bummed out before cracking a smile.

"No, no ..." She gets flustered.

He reaches for her. "No worries. It's cool how creative you are. I was just hoping to hang a little bit."

"Later?" she asks.

His grin confirms it.

Seeing how down in the dumps Ben is, I think he needs a friend. TJ and Emily are always there for me. I need to be here for Ben, like I was for Aaron. I talk to Graham with my eyes and encourage him to leave. Graham taps Jack.

"Wanna go shoot some hoops?"

"Let's do it."

Graham stands up. "See you later, Kai." He winks at me. I turn to mush and get all shy.

"Okay."

Ben hasn't touched a morsel of his food, not that I blame him. The pain radiating from him is so extreme it's cutting through me. He couldn't even enjoy a moment of peace on a picnic he helped create.

I lean in to him. "Hey, wanna, like, go for a swim or something?" I ask.

He lifts his eyes away from his uneaten sandwich.

He's so awkward and uneasy. I grab his hand.

"Come on."

Ben and I opt for a swim. After changing into our bathing suits, we head down to the lake. Walking behind him, I really get a sense of things, the big picture. I thought I was thin. Ben is probably 120 pounds soaking wet. At about five nine, that's flat-out scrawny. Sagging board shorts and a wrinkled shirt hammer home the state he's in. His outfit is a metaphor for his life. One big fucking mess.

We ease our way into the cool water. "Race you out to the float," I challenge him. He dives under and gets a jump on me. We swim toward the inflatable water trampoline.

He tags up a body's length before me. We climb onto the float, lying flat to catch our breath. He turns toward me.

"This was a good idea, Kai. Thanks."

Even if it's only for these few moments, the water washes away Ben's pain.

After we soak up the rays for a few minutes, the sun dries us off a bit. I roll over and leap into action. Jumping up and down, Ben is bouncing all over the place laughing his head off. I do a backflip over the edge into the water. Ben follows me with a belly flop. I splash water in his face when he surfaces.

We take turns doing flips and dives.

Jen was so right about the water. Soothes the soul.

"You want to take a break?" I suggest more than ask, noting his fatigue.

"Good idea. I don't have much energy," he answers.

"Eat more," I joke.

Kind of.

"I'm working on it."

We climb back on the floatie and sit side by side, legs touching, with our feet dangling in the water.

"I wish I could turn back time. I would never have gone to the science fair. In the scheme of things, it wasn't that important. Then there wouldn't have been a wreck," Ben shares.

"The accident sounded pretty horrific," I say, my eyes fixated on the lake, not wanting him to feel the obligation of eye contact. He's quiet, and I wonder if I've gone where I shouldn't have.

"Every day is a nightmare, Kai," he says finally. "Like, the realization that I'm really on my own. All I want is my family back."

Words lodge in my throat. What I want to do is wrap my arms around him and make it all better. For this one second, I'm not thinking of myself.

"While Cory is barely hanging on, both sides of my family are at war. My aunt is fighting to get custody of us even though we barely know her. She and my dad hardly ever spoke. My uncle is trying to keep us but he lost his youngest sister and the brother-in-law he played softball with every Wednesday night. He's in his own private hell. I look at Graham and Jack. Who's gonna teach me to be a guy like that? Now I don't even have my dad to help me."

"Oh, Ben. You don't need to be Graham or Jack. You're enough."

A tear sneaks down his cheek. I silently pray that I'm enough as well.

Chapter 19

I find Cass sitting on the rug in the middle of our cabin, cross-legged in front of a lavender candle, hands turned toward the ceiling with her index fingers and thumbs together. I start to tiptoe through the room but the creaking floorboards give me away. She opens her eyes.

"Sorry."

"It's okay, I'm done. Marco suggested meditation, so I thought I'd give it a try."

"Is it working?" I ask, crouching next to her. "It didn't for me."

"First day," she says, "so no idea. I figure it can't hurt. It's forcing me to stop worrying about what's going to happen next. My mom and the other kids have been living at Grandma's, and things seemed fine when I talked to them. But who knows, right?"

I note she did not say *sister*. In my mind, I'm hugging her for that.

"I keep waiting for the other shoe to drop," she adds.

"Maybe it's not going to this time," I try.

"I can't handle being let down yet again," she says.

Cass is so strong yet so fragile. Not being able to count on my mom has never entered into the equation. I relied on my sister but it wasn't because of an absent parent. It was my choice.

"Did you get some writing done?"

"Yeah, I was stuck on the chorus of the song and it hit me while we were talking about ups and downs."

"Totally clocked the flirt fest with Jack. What's that about?"

"I can't stop thinking about him. Not just his looks, though they don't hurt. It's the way he listens, the way he keeps eye contact when he talks to you. Like he isn't looking over his shoulder for someone better to walk by. Those are the guys at my school. But ... is that bad? I mean, we're not at a dating camp."

I'm wrestling with the same thing so I don't know what to say.

"Back home, a guy like Jack would never give me the time of day," Cass admits. "He's so hot and I'm so not."

I know what to say to that, at least: the truth.

"You're beautiful, and he's totally into you," I say adamantly.

"Come on, Kai, look at me. I have crazy hair and I'm not a size four."

"Who is and who cares? You're perfect just the way you are. Jen used to say that to me all the time."

As I say it, a light shines on my messy, broken self. Perfect in its imperfection.

* * *

When I fling open the bathroom door, wrapped in my rainbow-colored bath sheet, ready to get back to my guy talk with Cass, imagine the surprise on my face when I find *the* guy leaning in the doorway. Just one more thing that would never happen at home. It's like I woke up in someone else's life.

"Hi?"

Graham sizes me up, head cocked. "Hello. Bet you weren't expecting to see me. Nice outfit."

"It's the newest trend," I joke, totally embarrassed. Dripping hair, wrapped in terry cloth ... not exactly irresistible.

"Sorry to just show up but I didn't have your number. I was thinking we could hang out or something." He says it like it's no big deal.

"Let me get dressed," I manage.

"It's cool, I'll be out in front. No rush."

Cass swings her leg around, kicking the door closed. "Sorry I couldn't warn you. He knocked just as you were getting out of the shower."

I grab the first pair of shorts I see hanging over the chair and find a T-shirt in the top drawer. My brain goes from zero to eighty in full-on overthinking mode.

"Is this a date?" My voice is a whisper-screech. "No one dates at grief camp, do they?" Cass doubles over. I guess that's my answer.

Pulling myself together, I hear my sister's laugh, hear her encouraging me, *Go for it*. I look at my damp ponytailed self in the mirror and apply just a little bit of lip gloss. I don't want to look like I'm trying too hard. As an afterthought, I dab some vanilla-scented oil behind each ear then at the base of my throat. You know. Just in case.

"You look all kinds of adorable. Just go enjoy yourself."

"I'm not sure I remember how to do that," I admit, heading out the door.

Go for it.

I find Graham leaning against a giant pine tree a few steps away from Cabin Three holding two bottles of water, a bag of Flamin' Hot Cheetos and a bag of M&M'S, killing the jeans he's wearing. His white V-neck tee complements his untamed locks.

"No beanie?" I ask.

"I thought I'd dress up for our big date," he says. "I hit the vending machine."

Cute and likes junk food. Dark hair, deep blue eyes.

I'm swooning. At grief camp.

The campground is alive, teeming with little kids playing hide-and-seek. A volleyball game between the under-fifteens rages on in the sandpit we pass as we make our way toward the woods. We could be in Anywhere, USA, on summer vacation.

Graham and I bump shoulders as we move away from the campers and cabins toward the lake. I stumble on an oversize rock I didn't see, nearly taking a header. I grab the loop on the back of his jeans to save myself from falling.

"Are you okay?" he asks, stifling a laugh.

"Yeah, just a rock, I'm good." I blow it off even though I'm mortified. I haven't been around a guy other than TJ in ages. And Chris, well, he wasn't really anything other than a mistake. I've been staying in the friend zone since that whole debacle. But what do I have to lose? I've already lost the best thing in my life. I opt to keep my index finger around his belt loop and he doesn't seem to mind one little bit.

Graham guides me off the trail. "Careful, climb down here." He points to an alcove snugly hidden between two imposing evergreens down an embankment of dried pine needles and brush.

He explains, "I found this place the first day we got here. It's where I go to be completely alone."

He grabs my hand to help me down the hill. The feel of his warm skin touching mine gives me the tingles. He twists toward me.

"But now I don't want to be alone. I want to be with you," he says. He sets his phone next to us and the epic piano solo from Jen's Best of The Script's playlist fills the air. How could he know?

"Justin's favorite song," he says.

"It was one of Jen's, too."

Graham goes silent, getting lost in the lyrics.

"I love that part. I'm trying to walk through this hell for my brother. You know, be a champion."

Sitting with his back against the tree, he pulls me between his legs. I position myself with my elbows on his bent knees. I hear the rip of the Cheetos bag, then it appears over my shoulder.

"I love these." I grab a handful and pop them in my mouth, hoping the crunching isn't a turnoff. I breathe a sigh of relief when he returns the crunch.

"So did my sister," I add, thinking back on all those nights we stayed up watching movies. A smile creeps across my face. Jen would be so happy for me right now.

"Was Justin a junk-food guy?"

"Just the pizza obsession and he would be offended if you called it junk food. You would've liked him."

"If he was anything like you ..." I reach for his hand, which is resting by my side.

"He was more outgoing and likable."

Self-effacing.

"Oh, you're likable," I insist. Glad he can't see my face, I feel the burn from the blush. My flirt game could use some help.

He hands me his phone. "Pick a song."

I search his music and hit Play. The Beatles' classic "Let It Be" begins. "When I was twelve, my dad took me to a Beatles tribute concert. He told me that this song represents the light in all of us. No matter how much darkness there is, if we let it be, the light will find its way to us. Regardless of how bleak it might seem."

"Your dad sounds cool. He's got a legit point."

Maybe he does. It might be time to heed my dad's advice if I'm to move to a different place with Jen's death.

Maybe the answer is there is no answer.

I wonder if I can just let it be.

Graham surprises me when he places his lips on the nape of my neck, gently kissing it, sending so many new feels through me that I'm not sure what to do next.

"You make it so easy for me to open up," he says so lightly that I feel his breath on my ear.

I lean farther into him as he continues.

"The days and weeks after Justin died were all the same. Basically, intolerable. I couldn't stop going through all his stuff. The lacrosse shirts, his trophies, his everything. Just to have him around me."

"That's better than me. I was fixated on choosing the right outfit for Jen to be buried in, selecting the perfect prayer cards for her service. All the little things. I just had to get it all right, make it perfect. Nothing's ever perfect, is it?" I ask.

"This moment feels pretty darn close." His revelation catches me off guard. "I didn't expect this when I first got here," he throws in.

"Pretty much the last thing I imagined might happen." I stumble over my words.

"I never do stuff like this. My brother was that guy. He would go up to any girl, fearless, and just launch into conversation. Not me. With you, it's different."

I turn toward him and fall into his eyes. While I'm busy falling, Graham eases my hair out of the ponytail holder and runs his fingers through it, tucking it behind my right ear. Chills race from the top of my ear to the bottom of my toes and several places in between on the way down.

I wrap my legs around his waist. We're facing each other, not another soul in sight.

He slides his thumb to the corner of my mouth, leaning in to me in one fluid motion. His parted lips graze mine. Then he pulls away, leaving me wanting a whole lot more before he moves back in, nibbling on my lower lip before slipping his tongue into my mouth, making its way around like it's been here before. The longest, deepest kiss in my life is happening in the middle of the woods with a guy who is as broken as I am.

My sister died and I'm making out. Full disclosure: right this second, his tongue is winning the battle over my guilt.

By a long shot.

Even with Cheetos breath.

We move away from each other for a split second to catch our breath. His indigo eyes speak to me in a way I've never known. The kiss that follows is more heated and evokes sensations I didn't know existed. Love, lust and security collide.

Graham envelops me, holding me tight to his chest for a long time until the temperature drops and the sun disappears behind the clouds. There's a force field of magnetic energy between us.

His scruffy cheek tickles me. His chin rests softly on my shoulder, and his breath is hot against my flesh.

"You're saving me," he says, so close that my body trembles.

"You make me feel normal again."

If this is normal, I'll take it.

Chapter 20

For the first time since the Tuesday from hell, I awake refreshed. A check of the phone tells me I missed a late-night call from TJ, I have ten texts and I slept almost eight hours. Wait, I slept eight solid hours?

Cass is contorted in the most uncomfortable position, sound asleep. I've learned that she's one of those people who can sleep standing up. Lucky her. Careful not to make any noise, I roll over on my side and slip my journal out of the leather backpack.

I see the postcard I tucked in the inside pocket, back on day one. This time, I can't wait to see the handwriting I know is on the opposite side.

Found this in a shop outside of Paris. Thought of you. How could I not? I know how much you love Wilbur. Paris is just about as magic as this book. The food, the vibe, the everything. I'm loving it all. You'll see what I mean when you and TJ get here. xo JJ.

Knowing she was happy when she wrote this makes me think I can be happy, too. At least sometimes. At least today. Balancing my journal on my knees, I turn to a blank page to start my morning entry.

Today feels like it could be a pretty decent day. When I woke up the first thought I had was one filled with life, not death. Totally new concept. What is alive and well in my head has a name and it's Graham.

This makes me miss my sister even more. I'm desperate to talk to her, get her input. I counted on her ability to answer my questions. And I have a lot of questions.

What if my kissing ability didn't measure up to Graham's previous girlfriends? What if he doesn't think of me as a girlfriend? What if this is Chris all over again? What if this means nothing? I have to stop overanalyzing. I'm going to make this a good day. Hope.

Yeah.

That.

Progress.

* * *

Cass and I are the last to arrive for group. I scan the circle for Graham, and his smile takes my breath away, inviting me to throw caution to the wind. I head right for him, purposely brushing against his knee as I sit down. If anyone suspects anything's going on between us, they aren't letting on.

"Ping-Pong later?" Jack offers before we start. Like an incentive to get through this.

I glance at my boy to see if he wants to go. That's when Jack snickers, nailing me. The warmth rushes to my cheeks, making me full-on blush.

Marco breaks in. "When you are grieving, it's easy to get caught up in all the things you've lost. I want you all to visualize some things that you are thankful for. To remind you of hope. The first thing that pops in your mind. Kai, why don't you start?"

I don't even mind going first. "The way I feel today." I tilt my head and look sideways at Graham. "I didn't hate waking up."

My group needs no prompting, everyone follows suit.

"Kai," Graham says so matter-of-factly that my jaw drops open.

Jack elbows him. "Dude. So awesome."

Ben picks it up. "I'm thankful that my uncle brought me here and that he's fighting to keep me and Cory with him. I really hope he can make it happen."

After all this, Ben could get stuck in the middle of a custody battle. I can't even imagine.

Jack continues. "Thankful for my mom. There's not much left of my family, but she's the glue holding us together," he says. He nudges Cass. "Your turn."

With certainty, Cass answers, "All of this that we've been doing. I'm figuring out how to deal."

"I told you all of this would help you. If you'd trusted me on the first day, it would've saved you so much time stressing out," Marco teases.

People start laughing, of course.

I need to say something else that's on my mind. "I do feel guilty for not being consumed with Jen's death today," I say. "Like I'm betraying her memory somehow. But today, it doesn't hurt to breathe. I'm content."

"Kai, it's not betrayal to allow happiness back into your life. All your loved ones would want you to feel that again," Marco says.

"Do you really believe I'll be able to feel that?" Ben asks.

"With everything I have, buddy. You will never forget what happened but it will become part of your everyday landscape. Your parents will always be a part of you, but you will not always be in pain," Marco stresses.

"Being here, talking about it, has been a game changer for me," admits Jack. "I didn't want to burden my mom with how much I was hurting. Jeez, she lost her husband. I felt like I should man up but I couldn't."

"Men hurt. Men cry," Marco reassures him.

I see a noticeable relief on the faces of all three guys. It never occurred to me that the weight of the whole real-men-don't-cry notion would be so heavy.

I like the way this freestyle morning is shaping up, so I make an effort to keep the conversation going. "It's so bizarre. I have two best friends at home but I couldn't talk to them about what I was going through the way I've been able to do with you guys."

Marco nods. "Again, totally normal. Your friends want to be there for you but they have no frame of reference for all the things you are experiencing."

"Do you stay in contact with anyone from your group?" asks Graham. My stake in this answer is fairly high so I'm dialed into Marco's response.

"Every single one," he says.

I'm not gonna lie, those three words are a relief.

Then he starts our activity. "When you first came here, our group sessions revolved around your grief. Today, I want you to share thoughts of happiness about your loved one. Start to associate feel-good moments with them, not the pain of your loss."

I like this already. We each gather the photos we brought from home, just like the list instructed us to do, for this exercise. Opening my journal, I remove a few photos. Graham puts his hand in his back pocket and produces a dog-eared, worn picture, even though his most prized remembrance is neatly tucked over his head. Ben struggles with the sealed envelope he brought and Cass rustles around in a recyclable bag.

"I'd like to go first," she volunteers. Cass empties the contents of the bag in front of her.

I see happy.

I see hopeful.

"They aren't homemade but they are cookies. From the vending machine. I cleaned them out. And this is my grandma," she says, passing the picture around the circle for us to meet her. "It's from last Christmas, when we were baking cookies. I think it's time to have my first cookie since she died. With all of you."

Her eyes fill as she passes out yellow-and-blue bags of Famous Amos chocolate-chip cookies. Ceremoniously, she opens her bag and pops an entire cookie into her mouth. Then another. With each bite, I hope her pain fades away.

Jack hems and haws before he reveals a medal with a picture. I get to hold them first. His father looks so proud in the photo, in full-dress uniform.

Jack says, "This is my father's Purple Heart. You get one if you're wounded or killed in combat, and the soldiers who came to the funeral presented it to my mom. She gave it to me before I came here so I'd have my dad's courage with me. He was a hero."

Even Marco is unable to remain stoic. A teardrop slips down his cheek and he doesn't even bother to wipe it away. I really do like him.

I hand over a picture of my sister and me in Hawaii when I was about nine months old. I'm holding a red plastic shovel in one hand, a blue Otter Pop in the other, perched on top of her belly while she's sunbathing on an oversize beach towel in the backyard, slathered in sunscreen. I can almost smell the coconut.

As the photograph makes its way around the circle, I explain, "I was born in Honolulu. I guess I hated the grass and sand. I mean, I went full-on freak-out if a blade even grazed my feet. According to my family. I don't know why they'd lie about that. Anyway, Jen would let me sit on her so I didn't have to touch the grass. She always had my back."

Graham glides his hand into mine and squeezes it knowingly.

Ben unhooks the clasp on a manila envelope, digging out an eight-by-ten photo and turning it around for the group to see. It's his whole family in Hawaiian shirts, sporting sunburns and grins. I mean, these shirts are the kind that you make fun of when you see anyone wearing them, especially a whole family.

"Spring break. My dad surprised all of us with a trip to the Big Island. It was my mom's fortieth birthday. He wrapped the plane tickets inside a beach bag filled with everything she would need at the beach. She was so shocked she couldn't stop crying. My dad really never did stuff like that. They were supposed to go to Hawaii for their honeymoon, but my grandpa got sick so they had to postpone it. Then they had my brother and me so it got back-burnered. Dad swore he would never be one of those guys who made his kids wear matching shirts, ever." Ben busts up laughing.

"One afternoon my mom snuck down to the hotel gift store when we were surfing and bought us these." He points to the shirts. "A guy at the beach club took our picture. My dad thought it was pretty funny."

"You'll always have that memory," I say, channeling my father.

Graham unfolds the picture in his hand. "This is Justin and me the day he died."

They're decked out in their crimson-and-light-blue West Hill Academy lacrosse uniforms, looking ruggedly handsome. Justin is totally owning the Neff beanie that's currently fixed on the head of the boy who has stolen my heart. Justin is cracking up at whatever Graham has just said.

"We won the game and I was teasing him about his beanie. He loved this thing. He thought it got him girls. Maybe it did, but I doubt it. He did that just by being him. Everyone loved him, and so did I."

I return the squeeze, hoping it gives him the same relief. With my free hand, I wipe the tear that snuck out of his eye.

Marco claps his hands together. "It's a gorgeous day. The afternoon is all yours, folks. Art therapy after dinner."

"Circle up," Cass says.

I'm going to long for this hand hug when I get home.

* * *

Graham sends a group text after we all part ways.

Meet at the sandpit in ten.

Sounds so undercover. Cass and I show up and find Graham and Jack tossing a football around.

"What's going on?" I ask.

"We thought we'd play a little touch football. You know, teach Ben some ball skills," Graham says.

I shared my conversation with Ben with Graham. And he remembered. This guy.

When Ben arrives, he looks like he's been through the ringer.

"Hey, buddy. How about some touch football? I'll teach you all my moves," Jack offers.

Ben's eyes widen. "You know I'm not really much of a sports guy."

"I'm gonna make you one." Jack's easy smile does the trick.

"Keep your eye on the ball when I release it. Let it come to you."

The three of us pay close attention. Ben drops the first pass. He hangs his head a little, but that doesn't disguise his disappointment.

"No worries, you'll get the hang of it," Graham says, bending next to him. "Okay. Put your fingers on the laces." Graham positions the ball in Ben's hand. "Bring your arm back and up." Graham moves Ben's arm, teaching him the throwing motion.

"Show me what you've got." Ben lets the ball fly. It's not exactly the most accurate pass but Jack catches it, ensuring Ben's success.

"Yes!" Ben thrusts his fist in the air. He even smiles.

"All right, let's do this. I take Ben. You three defend," Jack calls out.

Graham huddles us up while Jack kneels down to show Ben how to get into a three-point stance and hike him the ball.

"Whatever you do, do not tackle him. Let him catch the ball," Graham whispers to the rest of us.

I couldn't fall any harder for this guy. But this can't be happening right now ... it's all wrong ... I could really use Jen to bounce this one off.

"He needs this way more than we do," he emphasizes.

If what I'm feeling is wrong, I don't want to be right.

Jack yells, "The end of the pit's a touchdown. Okay?"

We nod and line up. Graham hangs back to defend the goal. "You two rush the quarterback," he says, totally cracking up.

I point to Jack. "Coming for you." That grin he flashes is an unfair advantage.

From the shotgun position a few steps behind Ben, he yells, "Bring it. Hut, hut." Ben hikes the ball. It's a little wonky but Jack's skills easily keep the ball in play. Cass and I chase Jack in the backfield. He scrambles around like the pro he is.

"You'll never get to me," he teases, managing to dodge us. I'm totally trying to get to him, but the guy has mad foot skills. Jack signals Ben with his free hand.

Graham moves from side to side around Ben, tapping him, acting like he's all over him.

But Ben breaks free and Graham slows so he's at least two steps behind him. Ben runs closer to us, and Jack dumps the ball off lightly right into Ben's gut.

"Close your arms in, tuck the ball," Jack cheers him on. Ben takes off. Almost at the end of the pit, Graham touches him. Can't make it look like a gimme.

Jack rushes up to high-five Ben, and Graham fist-bumps him. "Nice fake, you got me."

I wish I could bottle the look on Ben's face. Pure bliss.

"Not gonna happen again," Graham promises as he walks away. Ben can't see the wide smile on my boy's face.

Ben joins in the smack talk. "We'll see. Let's get it, Jack."

Jack puts his hands on Ben's shoulders, telling him the next play in a hushed tone. Then he jukes back and forth in front of Cass and me. "You might catch me. Not."

This time, Jack lines up right under center. "Hut." Ben takes off as soon as the ball is in Jack's hand. Cass and I dive into Jack but not before he releases the ball. *Please let Ben score*, I think. He needs this.

Ben follows the ball with his eyes just like Jack instructed. It's like watching it in slow-motion. That's how it feels from here.

"Get under it!" Jack yells.

I hold my breath when Ben bobbles the ball. All Graham has to do is reach in and bat the ball down. He doesn't. Ben keeps possession, crossing the invisible goal line.

He lights up. An air of confidence encircles him. Maybe the goal line is a metaphor for his life.

Whoa.

Chapter 21

This morning after group Marco gives us a writing exercise to finish by tomorrow. Yeah, this one sucker-punches me. We have to write a letter to our loved one.

When he says those words, they elicit a few *Oh my fucking Gods*, with a side of nervous twitching from everyone in the group, especially me.

"The idea is for you to say what you didn't get a chance to say to them before they died," he says.

"Do we have to read them out loud?" I squeak, dying inside.

Thank you, Grief Gods. His answer is no.

Before dinner, Cass and I huddle on our beds. She has already filled an entire page of her notepad. I'm still staring at mine. All I've got is *Dear Jen*. I want to finish before Graham comes by, because we're in that make-the-most-of-every-second mode with the end-of-camp date creeping up on us. The thought of leaving him — and here — in a week is making me sick to my stomach. Just when we've found security here, it's almost time to go.

"The sucky thing is by leaving here, I lose Graham. Saying it out loud makes it even worse than thinking it. It reminds me of one of the prayer cards we saw at the funeral home. 'The Lord giveth and the Lord taketh away.' The Lord is unfaireth, if you ask me."

She laughs, though I'm really not joking.

"Oh, please. I see the way he looks at you. You two have a special connection."

"The losing-a-sibling connection," I reply, fending off the tears. After the other shit I've been through, I can't believe I'm crying, but there it is.

"It's way more than that. You can't deny that it's the thread tying it all together but that's okay. There's common ground whenever you care about someone."

"True." One word but it means a lot to me.

"He isn't going to allow a little distance to keep you guys apart. It's not like he's in New Jersey." Cass keeps the positive flying at me.

"It's not like he's in Fort Lauderdale, either. I can't stop thinking about all the girls at his school," I say, knowing the boyfriend of my dreams will be over an hour north of me in West Palm Beach.

"You guys will find a way. And, none of those girls are you."

I contemplate that while I peruse all the photos in my phone. There are hundreds. I've been documenting every moment since our first kiss. Graham giving me a piggyback ride through the woods. The two of us biting an ice-cream cone at the same time — what a mess that was. A selfie at sunset by the lake, my head resting on his shoulder. We're cute together. Really, we are. I come across a video Jack took of us spinning on the tire swing. I hear Graham laughing and me screaming. I play that a few times. His laugh is infectious.

I cannot get enough of it, especially after the dark times with no laughter at all.

Okay, I even have screenshots of our late-night texts. Reading them invites all the happiness in and I let it. I scroll to a thread he started one midnight last week.

Wish you were next to me.

We could build a blanket fort.

And never come out.

I would love that. xo

All the *x*'s and *o*'s back.

He signed off with:

You're the best thing that's ever happened to me.

Just rereading that gives me chills.

I don't want to forget a single second. My heart has been on ice for way too long.

I select a picture of the two of us with our arms wound tightly around each other, with me wearing his beanie. Our faces say it all. Love. Joy. Life. I group text the picture to TJ and Emily.

So, this is happening. Xo

I smile at the picture and wish I could send it to Jen as well. I do the next best thing. I send it to my mom.

I met someone pretty great. I can't wait for you to meet him.

Then I finally start this thing that Marco is twisting my arm to write. I lift my white letter-size pad, a black fine-tip pen in hand, and start to compose a letter to my sister. I'm überconscious of the shape of each letter I write. Careful not to be sloppy with my handwriting or my words — Jen would hate that.

It all matters.

Dear Jen,

I miss you so much. I keep hoping to see you when I walk into a room, around every corner, anywhere. But I don't. Then the hurt rushes back, not releasing me.

When you died, I wanted to die with you. I hated being left behind. Does that make sense? It was always you and me. All of a sudden there was just me and that wasn't enough.

So much has happened. Mom and Dad sent me to grief camp. I'm here now. I fought it at first but honestly I was a mess — a red-hot one, as you loved to say — spiraling so far out of control that I figured, why not? You told me to trust Mom, so I did. Turns out it was a good call.

At home, no one was talking about it ... I know: SURPRISE. I needed to talk about it more than I realized. All the kids here understand what I'm going through. Well, they don't get the suicide thing but they identify with the devastating loss. I'm heartbroken yet so furious with you, and it's a constant battle. You're gone. You did this to me. And I'm fucking mad, really fucking mad.

I hope that you aren't disappointed in my lack of ability to just be like, "Oh it's okay that you killed yourself on purpose, Jen." It's not.

Full disclosure, Mom took the pill bottles from your bathroom and I swiped a boatload. I don't know why you had all those meds. I guess I'll never know but there sure were a lot of them. I just don't know how to be me without you. I need your help, but you're not here. I can't articulate the depth of missing you. The things we were supposed to do

208

together. I mean, I even ditched school to spend time at the cemetery with you.

I wish so many things. That you were here. That I knew why you were hurting inside so much. That I would wake up and this wouldn't be. That I could put my arms around you one more time. That I wasn't going to be an only child for the rest of my life.

I'm working on forgiving you. That's the best I can do. None of this changes the fact that I will always love and miss you.

But. Still.

I'm pissed.

Really pissed.

Kai Bear.

P.S. I love you.

I fold it neatly, placing it next to me just as a flurry of texts arrives.

My mom. *Oh, Kai. Jen would love this. I do, too.*

I never talk to Mom about guys. That was my sister's department.

TJ. *Your smile made me cry. And, he's hot. Really hot.*

I crack up, knowing he's freaking out right about now.

Em. *That's what happy looks like. Love you. Em*

* * *

I inch as close as possible to Graham without being under his skin, counting down the number of hours — about 168, give or take a few minutes — that we have together before we leave what has become my refuge. Oh, and the very first place I fell in love. The absolute last place in the universe you'd expect to find it.

We're hidden away in our special nook in the woods with the world locked out, my compact frame tucked under his arm like it was meant to be there. I hand him the first in my deck of Jen's postcards.

"That's incredible," he says, checking it out.

"Barcelona. Sagrada Família. She loved Gaudí's architecture. Flip it over."

"You want me to read it?"

"I want you to know her," I say gently. He flips the postcard over. Just the sight of her handwriting moves me in a way nothing else ever will.

I've been eating my way through Spain. Tapas is the answer to everything. I miss you like crazy. Next time, I'm bringing you with me. Xo JJ

He repositions me so I'm closer to him, rubbing my arm.

"It kills me that there will never be a next time."

His calming hand strokes my shoulder tenderly. I draw another postcard from the pile and can't help but giggle.

"The Lindt chocolate factory in Zurich. She loved candy, especially all things chocolate." Turning it over to read it to him, I say, "This is vintage Jen."

Ok, tried over a dozen different chocolates but found something that changed my life. No shit. It's a truffle. When you bite into it, an explosion of creamy chocolate fills your mouth. Better than sex. Not kidding. Bringing some home ... if they make it. xo JJ

"I'm not sure about that better-than-sex thing. Were they?" he asks. Kind of a sly way to find out if I'm a virgin.

"They never made it home. However, I can say with certainty they have to be better than the one and only time I ever had sex."

Graham holds on to me tighter. I'd give anything to get that day back. But it doesn't work that way. No do-overs for bad-judgment sex.

Somehow I want to tell him more. "I fell for an older guy's BS moves. It lasted about a minute, the relationship and the sex, then he dumped me. By text."

"What a piece of shit." He kisses my forehead, gently resting his head next to mine. In the tenderest voice, he cements his place in my heart. "I would never do that to you. Ever.

"Can I ask you something?" he asks so sweetly I feel the tingles.

"Anything," I say.

"Your sister signs her name 'JJ.' What's that about?"

That's not what I thought he was gonna ask. "When I was two and a half, she giggled at the way I said Jen, so I'd repeat it over and over to get her laughing. It worked every time. Jen Jen. It just stuck as we grew up. I was the only one who called her that," I explain.

His eyes mist up along with mine. I think I need a subject change.

"Tell me something fun about Justin. I want to know everything."

He perks up, tapping his foot against the side of my shin.

"He loved messing with people, pranks were his thing. Like, one time he put itching powder on my jockstrap before practice. As soon as I started to sweat ... well, you can imagine. The whole team was in on it, even Coach. While I was freaking out, he was rolling on the ground laughing his ass off. For real, I thought I was coming out of my skin."

I can't help cracking up.

"Really?" He gets all fake indignant.

"Sorry ..."

"It took a twenty-minute ice-cold shower to get all of it off." He tries to look pouty but his smirk keeps sneaking through.

I muss his hair up. He wrinkles his nose.

"Why do I think you got him back?"

A grin spreads across his chiseled jaw.

"I may have filled one of his AXE sprays with vinegar. When he doused himself, it wasn't pretty."

"I better watch my back with you."

I stroke his hair. I kiss his cheek softly before going nose to nose with him, our eyes locking.

"Promise me we'll figure this out so we can see each other after we leave here," I say, trying not to sound like a clingy girlfriend.

"Kai?"

I turn to face him. His eyes are angelic, face inches from mine. Our arms brush up against each other.

"You make it better for me." He doesn't say what *it* is, because I know. I know.

"Same."

TJ pops into my head — that word is our bond. But it also bonds me to this boy, who's been brought into my life by death.

"It's just that I never thought I'd feel anything like this, my heart was so closed and broken." I can't believe how exposed I am. But I don't know how not to be with him.

The expression in his eyes is just such that my heart swells and my crush takes a wild turn.

"I love you, Kai."

You know when your face does that thing when someone utters the words *I love you?*

That happens.

"Same."

His lips caress my face with delicate kisses before his tongue finds my open mouth. As we're wrapped around each other, his soft lips kiss me harder and harder to the beat of my pounding heart.

I could kiss him forever.

Chapter 22

My mom just sent me a text to tell me that the gap-year idea is not dead. It's not a sure thing but Dad put it back on the table. Such a lawyer. We're negotiating my life.

I'm flipping out right now and talking to myself. "Europe, here I come. Maybe. I can't believe it."

I text back in all caps. YOU ARE THE BEST.

It's a lot but I can't help myself.

My mind is racing a hundred miles an hour. I have a shot. After senior prom, I *might* be going to Italy. Or Spain. Or Ireland.

Wait. Prom.

Graham and me at prom. With TJ and Em.

The sound of Cass opening the door stops my spin. I see the journal in her hand. *Oh that.* The sight of it deflates my bubble.

So caught up in my head, I almost forgot about today's task. *Almost.*

"Ready to do this?" Cass asks.

Not really, but Marco has been adamant — more like mili-
tant — about sticking to the journaling plan, and it's working so I'm
not arguing for once. Today we have to write about the things we
miss the most about the person we lost. Usually Cass and I retire to
our own corners, but tonight we choose to lie down on our throw
rug with pillows under our heads, right next to each other.

"My grandma used to put her pillow next to mine when I was
younger and couldn't fall sleep. It worked every time. It was our
thing. Or one of our things, actually. We had so many of them — I
never realized until she died. You know?" Cass says.

Yeah, I know.

"Jen and I had movie night. It was usually *Pitch Perfect* if we were
feeling the funny. *The Notebook* was the go-to cry-your-eyes-out
choice. We could quote both movies verbatim yet it never grew old.
We mixed plain M&M'S with SkinnyPop Popcorn for the perfect
salty-sweet combination. Our version of trail mix. I really miss that,"
I admit.

I open my journal to get started. Cass does the same. Together
makes it better, more bearable.

*Our writing assignment today is to jot down what we miss
the most about the person we lost and direct it to them. Here
you go, Jen. I miss you most when I hear any song by The Script.
In fact, I miss all your music texts. You were my music guru.
I miss you most when something like this thing with Graham
is happening and I don't have my sister to text WTF? I miss
you most when I think about never having a movie night again.*

215

I miss you most when I thumb through all the postcards you sent me and realize I will never go to the mailbox and see your handwriting again. I miss you most when I remember I'll never be someone's little sister. I miss you most at night right before I fall asleep when I close my eyes and remember that when I open them again, you will still be gone.

There's not enough paper or ink in my pen to write it all down. It's just that I miss everything about you. Xo Kai.

I glance over the top of my journal, wondering what Cass is writing about her grandmother. I'm just about to ask her but the crease between her eyes tells me she is in the zone. It's cool to be together but sometimes you just have to be alone with your thoughts and feelings. I'm okay with that.

* * *

The morning sun shining through the window isn't a bad way to wake up especially because it means, well, Graham. As soon as I throw off my sheet, Cass pops out of the bathroom clad in workout tights, a racer-back tank and running shoes.

"Run?"

"No thanks, I'm meeting Graham later."

"Bring your lip balm," she says, all singsong-like as she leaves, slamming the cabin door behind her.

She makes a good point. His lips on mine will definitely be happening. As much as possible before I leave, I need to bank all the kisses. I start digging around for my Fresh Sugar balm in my bag and — I stop. It's Jen's bag, not my bag. So odd that that wasn't my first thought when I touched it. I run my hands over the distressed leather she loved. The sun shining through our front window glints off something shiny. Intrigued, I dig deeper into the bag. When my fingers reach the object, I freeze. It may as well be a snake. I remember exactly what it is. I take it out and set it down on my pillow next to me.

I'm not sure I want to deal with this now. But I still can't find the lip balm. Instead, I unearth a note from my mother, written on her real-estate stationery. She must have snuck it in before she left. I read: *Kai, I keep thinking we'll find answers in the little things. I love you, Mom.*

I put Mom's note off to the side and pick up the box again. I need to be brave. I mean, this whole thing is about being brave. I was brave enough to come here, and it was just what I needed. And who's afraid of a Christmas gift, anyway? I stare at my sister's handwriting on the gift card. As I hold the box in my shaking hand, I almost, *almost* feel my sister's delicate hand take mine, gently urging me to open it right this second. I heed her advice, like I always have.

Taking my Swiss Army knife off the desk, I select the longest blade next to the mini-scissors. With the precision of a surgeon I slit the Santa along the fold where the tape seals it, careful not to tear the shiny holiday paper.

No one, I mean no one, loved Christmas like my sister and since I was her shadow, I feel the exact same way. She and I started the countdown to Christmas right after my birthday in October. We started playing Christmas carols on the first of November and didn't stop until New Year's Day.

Untying the brown twine that holds the card on the bright red bow, I cram the card inscribed *To Kai. Love You, JJ* inside the outer pocket of the backpack. The long tan gift box is from Blue Windows, an artsy jewelry store on a side street near the beach, next door to my favorite vintage-T-shirt store. Inside, on a bed of red tissue paper, is the most beautiful necklace I've ever seen, a sterling-silver chain with a circular medallion. Hammered in the middle are the words: *A journey of a thousand miles must begin with a single step.*

I've gotta tell Graham about this.

Meet up now? K

Definitely. At our place writing my letter to Justin.

Our place.

Be there in ten. Xo K

I slip a David Bowie tank top over my head.

Can't wait. So many xo's G

The response flusters me in all the best ways. I cradle the necklace safely in my hand, leaving the confines of Cabin Two. I bob and weave around a cluster of gigantic rocks. Tromping through the woods, I'm careful not to drop the precious gift that was last held by my sister's loving hands. I can just picture her in the store mulling it over like she did with everything she bought. Trying it on to see how it looked. Checking herself out from every angle. Lining it up next to other choices. Jen loved choices in condiments, accessories and life.

She took such care selecting things for people she loved.

I know she chose this saying for a reason. Her fixation on quotes, in books, in letters: every single word counted. I think about the journey. I wish I knew where the fuck it was going to take me. And Jen, well, she didn't even bother to finish her journey. Maybe mine will be enough for both of us. It's a new thought to go with my necklace.

Graham is lost in thought when I arrive, drinking a can of Coke, with Justin's hat tucked tightly over his ears. One thing about the woods, you can't exactly surprise someone. The crunching of the dead leaves and the *Oh shit* when you turn your ankle on a pinecone give you away.

He twists around and flashes the grin I've fallen hard for. "Hey you."

"Hey yourself. How's the writing coming along?" I lean down and kiss him, acting like I've done it a million times before.

"Can I read you what I've got so far?" he asks.

I plop down next to him, knee to knee, setting my hand on his leg, hoping he feels my love. "Of course."

Clenching the piece of paper so tightly I pray he doesn't tear it, he breathes in the crisp air and reads:

"'Dear Justin. Bro, I am so sorry I wasn't there to help you get out of the car. I wish it were me instead of you. You'd know how to work this all out. Navigate all this aftermath. My truth is that I don't know how to be me without you. Growing up, I looked up to you. I followed your lead on everything and that worked for me. This doesn't. It's all so fucking unfair. I know we never really said it but I hope you know how much I loved you.'"

His long eyelashes flutter, batting away the tears.

"'I counted on you every day. On the field and off. I'm gonna see if Coach will let me wear your number next season. I promise you I'll spend the rest of my life making you proud of me. Your brother always, Graham.'"

He buries his beanie-wearing head into my chest and lets out all that has been bottled up since day one. He was so closed off and apathetic. Now the guy I'm holding is open and compassionate. He needed this camp as much as I did.

Graham lifts himself off my lap, rubbing his face dry with the bottom of his West Hills Academy Lacrosse T-shirt. The vulnerability on his face reminds me of everything I love about this guy. We're on this journey together.

"Is that okay?"

"It's beautiful, Graham."

"I'm going to leave it on his headstone for him when I get home."

I lean in and graze his cheek with my lips. "He would love it and be so proud of you for facing this down."

For a few brief moments, we stay still, taking in the beauty around us. His hand finds my hand, which is still clutching the necklace.

"What's this?"

"Jen left wrapped Christmas gifts for each one of us in her closet. My parents found them when they were packing up her apartment. I've had it here since we arrived at camp, but I only opened it today."

"That's intense," he says, securing his arm around my waist.

"When she picked this out for me, her mind was already made up," I say. Somehow that idea is hitting home right now. She never wavered. Truly, there was nothing we could have done.

Now I'm the one getting teary. "She bought our Christmas gifts early since she never planned on celebrating another holiday. She really did want to die."

Graham gently takes the necklace from me and reaches, his hand lightly touching my skin, to fasten it around my neck. The charm falls perfectly between my collarbones.

"'A journey of a thousand miles must begin with a single step,'" he reads. His face twists. "Let's be honest, that first step might suck, but Jen's right. It's really about the journey."

"Profound, right?" I say.

"Light-at-the-end-of-the-dark-tunnel profound," he points out.

"I'm grateful that you're part of the journey."

"Same." He rubs his finger on the charm, then takes my face in his sturdy hands. "I'm glad I'm the one walking right beside you."

Chapter 23

Nearing the finish line brings with it a plethora of emotions and anxieties. What is unfolding in front of me is level-ten ridiculous. It's picture day at grief camp. I really have grown to love this place but they've taken things one step too far. This isn't fucking yearbook.

And just like the day we took junior pictures for the yearbook, my hair isn't cooperating.

At all. God, all of this.

There's Cass with every single hair looking perfect even spiky while mine is, well, all over the place. Of course. She's Emily twin and I'm the messy sidekick.

"You look great," Cass tries. She can see me stressing. How long will this picture hang on the wall when we're gone anyway? However, there's some consolation. The two things that are perfect are my shirt and my necklace, both from Jen. That mellows me out a little bit.

"You know, Cass, when we got here, I couldn't comprehend all the smiles and optimism radiating from the pictures in the rec hall. Now, I can."

The people in those photos felt like I do now. I can't wait to go home. I've missed Duke so much even if he does hog the bed. TJ already has a full beach day planned with jet skis and Ozzy's. Guessing Fireball might find its way into our summer plans. This time for toasting, not numbing.

But Graham.

The knot in my stomach tightens.

Several of the counselors are rounding up kids for group photos that will soon be added to the wall. Laughter permeating the campgrounds. No scheduled activity other than fun. Cass and I join the guys and Alison under one of the shady trees.

Graham spots our fearless leader. "Hey, Marco. Over here."

Marco ambles over, all smiles, wearing a UCLA baseball hat.

Graham leans in to me. "I'm making it right."

I can't wait for my parents to meet him. They're going to love him just like I do.

"Huddle up, you guys." My boyfriend takes charge. "Let's build a pyramid."

"Cool idea." Alison throws in her two cents. She's got her camera at the ready.

"I'm not big on heights," Ben says.

Jack lightly slaps him on the back. "We got you."

"That's what my group did. Our picture is near the back door of the rec center." Marco gets nostalgic.

I bump Graham. "Score."

"Jack, Marco and I will be the bottom row. Cass and Kai, take the middle. It's gonna be an epic picture but we need you in the top spot, Ben. Conquer your fear, you can do it," Graham encourages him.

Well played.

"Dude, you can totally do it," Jack chimes in.

Marco and Jack flank Graham. I help Cass brace herself, one foot on Jack's back, the other on Graham's. Ben steadies me. If Ben's apprehensive, he isn't letting on. Alison lends him a hand as he balances himself on Cass and me before she starts shooting pictures.

I think about the significance of this pyramid. We built a foundation starting that very first day. We've continued to build our trust in one another, we've confided in one another. And now we're stacked perfectly, holding one another up.

I should try this with my parents.

* * *

Camp smells like the inside of a barbecue restaurant. Smoky meat smells fill the air along with the pungent odor of bubbling sauce. Corn on the cob is packing the grills with sweet rolls just begging to be buttered.

Graham and I are the only two from our group still in line for food. Aaron races up, leaving his dodgeball game to greet me. "Kai, Kai!!"

He runs into my arms and I twirl him around while he squeals with glee. When I stop spinning him, he wraps his legs around my waist. His hair is damp from sweat, his grin showing off a missing tooth.

"You lost a tooth, buddy?"

"Yeah, the tooth fairy came last night. I can't believe he found me."

I put my forehead to his. "Just like Santa. They can always find you. It's part of their magic.

"Aaron, this is Graham."

Graham throws his hand up to high-five him. Aaron answers it with gusto. His hand is a quarter the size of Graham's but there's still a loud smack.

"There you are," we hear Melia say, approaching us. "Let's get some food, little guy," she says, taking Aaron into her arms and walking with him to the little kids' picnic table.

"How do you know that kid?"

"I met him last week when I was on a walk. His mom had cancer. He was so withdrawn from the group. I gravitated to him. We sat together while he painted a picture for me. It felt so good to do something for someone else. Not to talk about me or my feelings. Making him feel happy made me happy."

"Kai, you were so amazing with him. His eyes lit up when he saw you."

The compliment makes me slightly embarrassed, but it does fill me with joy.

"For the record, you've done plenty for all of us, especially me." He soft-smiles at me.

Melting me into a pool of all the swoons and feels.

* * *

Today's one-on-one with Marco has me unsettled. Group therapy has been a challenge but at least I know what to expect from that. This one-on-one, not so much. I've been dreading it since I read about it in the welcome packet on the first day. Graham walks with me to Marco's cabin clenching my hand in his, knowing my apprehension.

"You'll be fine, Kai."

"Easy for you to say, you haven't gone yet," I tease.

Kind of.

"Jack said it really helped him. It's just another tool to help us move forward. It's all good. We aren't gonna have this safety net much longer," he reminds me. Stopping just outside Marco's cabin, I turn toward Graham, whose dreamy eyes reassure me.

"Wish me luck."

"Luck." He laughs, letting my hand drop. "I'll be here when you get out. Kai, you got this."

I shake my head as I knock on the door. "Come on in, it's open," Marco yells from inside.

"Sit wherever you like, make yourself comfortable." I take inventory of Marco's cabin. Two oversize shabby chairs and a worn leather couch decorate his space. A picture of a stunning woman holding the hand of a very young Marco is taped to his wall.

"My mom before she got sick. Isn't she beautiful?" With each syllable, I know his loss is every bit as deep as mine.

"You look just like her, Marco." I make him blush.

He waits until I sit. I cross my legs, tucking them up in the chair. Marco hands me a bottle of water and sits down across from me.

"Kai, this is not going to be so bad. Think of it like a final exam with no grade involved."

He laughs. I don't.

And then there's this awkward silence that I feel the need to fill.

"Something's been bugging me and it isn't going away and camp is almost over. I just can't seem to let it go."

"You can tell me anything."

I look at the floor. "I just don't understand how someone like Jen would want to die. Why? I still don't know the answer."

Marco pauses. "Seriously," he asks, "why is that so important?"

"It just is."

He puts his fingers together and leans toward me. "Honestly, Kai, no one really gets answers. Why did Ben walk away from the accident unhurt? Why didn't Graham go with Justin? Things happen. You're learning to understand your feelings. You're validating all your anger and sorrow. The hardest thing is accepting that you just can't know."

It's the one thing I really wanted from grief camp, and the one thing I'm not getting. "That's what I can't wrap my head around," I say.

"You will. I promise."

I look at his photo. His mother, gone. He said she was sick, so that's his answer, I think. But why did she get sick? Can he ever really know?

I can keep on asking. I can keep not knowing. Or, like the Beatles song, I can let it be.

In this moment, I give in to belief.

Belief in Marco.

Belief in the process.

Because I have to.

Marco cocks his head slightly.

"You know, Kai, you've come a long way since you first got here. You've shown incredible strength. You'll need all of that when you leave here."

Please let him be right and please let that strength follow me back to Fort Lauderdale.

"I was so angry when I left ..." I start to say. "My parents just disappeared." I'm angry now, too. "Why didn't they do something?"

Marco's voice stays calm. "Kai, your family didn't go anywhere. The only one missing is Jen. Parents don't always know what to do, and your parents brought you here. They needed help in helping you."

"Why would Jen do this to me? To us?" Maybe this time he'll tell me.

Patiently, he replies, "She didn't do this to you or your parents. Jen did this to herself, then it affected all of you. The domino effect. Many people who kill themselves are one person on the outside and another on the inside. That's why so many families never see it coming."

"So what do we do?"

"Come together with your parents. Accept. Forgive."

I study him while I allow those loaded words in.

"I'm not sure I know what you mean."

"You just have to accept that it happened and there was nothing anyone could have done. Not you. Not your mom or your dad. Then you need to work on becoming a family again. You all did the best that you could at the time. You lost your sister, they lost their child. Now you can do a little better."

"But they still had me and they forgot that," I snap.

"Suicide cripples families, and yours was no exception. You need to forgive them."

I sigh. "Okay, so how do I do that?"

"There are a few simple exercises I think might help."

I have to try. "Hit me."

"Make a list of the way your parents hurt you. Visualize forgiving them. Over and over. Release the anger. Then burn the list."

I can do that. And maybe take it one step further. I say, "And do the same for myself?"

"You got it," Marco says. "And then you talk to them. Not about Jen. Just talk. The words will build the relationship back to where it needs to be."

My mind races to the pained expression on my father's face when he left here and the way my mother rubbed my sister's bracelet like she could feel her.

"I think I can do that."

"I know you can, Kai."

Chapter 24

I wake up to the smell of freshly brewed coffee. In my cabin. Except we don't have a coffeepot, we don't even have coffee.

If my eyes aren't playing tricks on me, I see Cass in her pajamas standing next to my bed with a cup of caffeine and a glazed donut.

"Happy last day of grief," she jokes.

"Wouldn't that be nice?" I say, propping myself up in my bed. Cass hands me the cup of piping-hot caffeine goodness.

"Vanilla creamer, just the way you like it. I seriously don't know how you drink that junk. It's artificial with no nutritional value whatsoever. You should try soy milk."

"That will happen the day after never. Hey, did you go to the cafeteria in your pajamas?" I ask, realizing she's dressed for bed.

"Like it matters." She laughs.

I prop myself up against my pillow. Cass plops down on my bed, using my beloved throw to cover her feet.

I sip my morning surprise. Liquid heaven.

"How are you doing about leaving?" Cass asks.

"That's all I've been thinking about. It's the end of one chapter and the beginning of another. Surrendering the grief. That part I'm good with. Giving up seeing Graham and all of you on a daily basis, I absolutely am not. You?"

"There's no one at home I can talk to. It's scary," she says. "We won't have the group to lean on."

"You know we'll stay in contact no matter what comes up. We can talk, email, text, Skype. Friendship knows no distance. You heard Marco about his group." I lean over and embrace Cass, hoping I believe all that.

She shoves me away playfully.

"Sorry I'm getting all Hallmarky on you."

"I get it." She jumps up and heads over to her suitcase, starting to pack. I've learned over the last few weeks that she's not much for sitting still. Like my head, her body never shuts off.

She puts some music on her phone, dancing around carefree as she packs. Something I don't think she would've done that first day no matter how talky she was. Now there's a freedom and confidence that rule her.

"How do you think it's gonna be with your parents?" she asks as she folds her clothes.

"I can't wait to see them. Our last few calls have been more open. Even my dad has been more talkative. They've been going to therapy the entire time I've been here."

"Just like you. You can help each other just like we all did."

I never thought of it like that. Maybe we needed to separate to come back together.

"It seems like we just got here." I roll off the bed, taking a bite of sugary goodness, gathering my clothes from the floor and stuffing them into my duffel bag. My mom will probably have a heart attack when she sees this packing job. But it's no different from my room. No one said organization was part of grief camp. I wrap one of my shirts around Aaron's picture of Duke.

My eyes land on the framed crocheted quote on the wall.

Only when it's dark enough, you can see the stars.

I must have been lingering and staring for a while. Cass slinks up and plants her fingers firmly on my shoulder.

"I've been obsessing on this every morning since we checked in," she says.

"Me, too," I say quietly. "I think that's what this has all been about. Getting through all of the darkness to see the light."

"Will it ever be okay again?" Cass wonders.

"It depends on how you define *okay*," I say, with a hint of humor. "At least it won't suck as bad."

* * *

Hanging smack in between two giant pine trees, Graham and I lie in a white mesh hammock. I can't believe we've walked by this every single day and never jumped in. It's like lying on a pillow of air.

Floating.

"I'm so glad we skipped lunch and came out here," I say.

"I want to spend every minute with you before we go home." Pretty sure my whole body just broke out in a smile.

We've taken up residence in the hammock, my head at one end, his at the other, legs intertwined in the middle. So natural and right. He writes in his journal while I read *Franny and Zooey*, again. I reach next to my waist and grab his foot because I can. He sets his journal on his chest. I can tell by the glint in his eyes that he has an idea. A closed-mouth smile glides across his face.

"I have an idea. Something I've been thinking about for the last two weeks."

He's got my undivided attention.

"Let's apply to be junior camp counselors next summer. I talked to Marco about it after I saw you with that little boy." His eyes get wide as he continues. "We'd get to spend the entire summer together. You know, help other kids just like us. It could be our thing."

I flash back to Aaron and hope fills me. Like head to toe, not just a little bit. A lot.

I grab his foot again and give it a squeeze. "Our thing. I like the way that sounds."

"Thought you might."

He starts to sit up, nearly toppling both of us out of the hammock and onto the ground.

"Hey, are you trying to kill me?" I try to act all irritated but we both know I'm so not.

Steadying himself, he crawls up toward my end of the hammock, using the croqueted rope holes to get to me.

"What am I gonna do with you?" I tease him.

"I can think of a few things," he says, his grin peppered with sexy.

I shake my head but I'm thinking the very same things, I'm certain of it.

"So you know the day I went to play basketball with Jack?"

I nod. "Yeah."

"I kinda lied. But for a really good reason."

I'm a little peeved. "Not big on lying."

There's that damn smirk again. My inner Kai begs me to resist.

"You're cute when you're trying not to look pissed about something you have no idea about," he states, messing with me.

I raise my eyebrows. "Spit it out."

He plucks a woven leather bracelet from the side pocket of his olive cargo pants.

"Jack and I did play basketball, but I cut out early to make this for you."

Melting.

"When you look at it, you can remember our first summer together. Know it's not going to be our last." He takes my wrist and ties together the strands of leather on each end of the bracelet. "I'll always be with you."

This. Guy.

"You like it?"

Does he really have to ask?

"No, I don't like it." I let him sweat for a nanosecond, then plant a fat kiss on his dreamy lips. "I love it."

He locks his arms around me so tightly that a piece of paper couldn't fit between us. We stay that way for so many breaths, I'm lulled into a calm. When we finally break apart, we lose ourselves in each other's stare. I fiddle with my bracelet, then ease my head onto his broad shoulder, wishing I could stay there forever.

But I can't.

* * *

There's final, and then there's final.

The final that brought me here differs greatly from the final before me. For our last afternoon group session, we all meet at the rec center but instead of working on a banner — something that's apparently a Tree House tradition — Marco surprises us with a different closing exercise.

"We're taking a hike down to a stream that runs into the lake. Our last activity will take place there."

"Sounds good to me." Graham grabs my hand without hesitation as we follow the others into the lush forest.

I fall into step with him. Walking without talking is just what I need at this moment. Getting the opportunity to absorb the quiet, endless beauty around me one last time. To give thanks for all that the past four weeks have afforded me. For bringing love into my life at the worst time imaginable. I look at Graham and when he catches me — and grins back — my knees feel like they might buckle.

Stealth, I am not. To be fair, I'm new to this whole boyfriend thing.

The sound of snapping branches and crunchy leaves beneath our shoes is a constant reminder of how fragile we all are. At any moment, life can snap you in half, crumbling you in pieces, sending you and your world reeling.

"The stream is just up ahead," Marco announces.

As we near our destination, I can hear the babbling sound of water and the breeze in the leaves. A symphony of nature.

"Wow, this is beautiful," I hear Cass say. When we catch up to her, I see exactly what she's referring to: A crystal-clear torrent of water splashing as it hits rocks embedded in the side of the stream. Stones of all sizes and shapes, some submerged completely, others clearing a path in the shallow part of the river.

Marco sets the cooler he's been carrying on a thick bed of discolored pine needles. As he removes the top, revealing five golden sunflowers minus their stems, we all take notice.

"Gorgeous," remarks Cass.

He points out to the stream. "See the rock path into the water?"

"Yeah," we say in unison. He doles a flower out to each of us as he talks. I'm struck by the coarse base of the flower and the hair on what's left of the stem. The bright green moss that covers the sides of the rocks at the water's edge makes the stones look almost iridescent.

The air is so fresh with pine that I can flashback on Christmas and Jen.

"We're going to walk across the stones, then each of you is going to release a sunflower into the stream for your loved one. It's a letting-go ceremony. Let go of your grief, anger or whatever it is that isn't allowing you to move forward. Not move on, move forward. There's a big difference," Marco says knowingly. "And sunflowers symbolize loyalty, which you will always carry for the person you lost."

Ben sighs. He asks, "If we aren't ready to let go, can we just say something we miss?"

"Whatever you need to do to take a step in the right direction, forward. Like the grief process, there's no right or wrong way to do this."

Marco continues, "We'll walk out as a group. The rocks are slippery so watch your step. Then one at a time, you'll say what you are letting go of and release your flower."

We pile our backpacks away from the water and follow Marco cautiously, careful not to tumble in. Since I'm bringing up the rear, I stop and take a 360-degree look around.

Just being out here for such a magnificent day. The deep blue sky radiant with the sun's rays, not a cloud in sight. The sun reminds me of Jen's smile, the way it lit up a room. The water meandering through the woods emptying into the nearby lake with a gentle ease. The kind of ease Jen brought to me. The bubbling stream reminds me of life being fluid, ever-changing. The biggest change being that my life will no longer include Jen.

We join Marco near the center of the cluster of rocks and huddle up for one of the last times. The lump in my throat is real.

"Who'd like to go first?" Marco asks.

I almost fall off my rock when Graham speaks up.

"I will." He pauses, gazing out into the vast openness.

"I'm letting go of all of the guilt I've been carrying about not being in the car with Justin. If I had been with him, my parents would have lost both of us. Letting go of guilt, holding on to you, bro."

So confident.

So proud.

He's got a captive audience as he bends down and places his flower on top of the water. He kneels down like he's saying a prayer as he watches the water take the flower and the guilt away.

Cass speaks up next. "I'm letting go of the notion that we will never be a family without my grandmother. I've been so preoccupied with losing her that I forgot to be grateful for all that I still have."

She kisses the petals of the sunflower before leaning down and releasing it into the gurgling water, watching it float downstream.

"I'm going to try to let go …" Jack stops to chuckle as he exaggerates *try*. At least he's being honest. He continues. "Of all that I didn't say the day my dad deployed. Writing in the journal forced me to remember all the awesome things my dad and I did together when he was home this last time. He took me to a Braves game, we went four-wheeling on ATVs. Just hung out. He knew I was proud of him and loved him. Yeah, that."

He stoops down over the rushing water and lays his dad's flower gently down in the stream. With his back shuddering, he stays in that position long enough to indicate someone else should go ahead. He might be there awhile. Cass kneels beside him, gently moving his head to her shoulder.

Ben and I exchange a look. I turn my palm up and shrug.

"Go ahead, Ben." I'm avoiding this as long as possible.

"I'm going to let go of the blame. I blamed myself for my brother being in the car. But my parents made him go, not me. Just like they forced me to go to his swim meets when I didn't want to. That's what families do. I know it's no one's fault. It was an accident. A terrible accident. That's all." Droplets of sadness stream down his pale face and he wipes his cheek with the inside of his *Calculus: yes, it is rocket science* T-shirt.

I love this kid.

No backpedaling now, it's obviously my turn. The pressure on me is so intense that I feel I might combust.

I just have to get this right.

Like the prayer card.

Like the outfit.

Like the casket.

All the last things I would do for my sister.

I exhale what could quite possibly be the world's deepest breath.

"I'm releasing the anger I have toward my sister. I didn't know it was okay to be mad at someone for dying, but I was. Mad that she chose to kill herself. Mad that she picked death over me. Now I realize it's not that simple. She picked death over a life that was too hard for her to live. I can't be mad at her anymore for that. I just can't."

I kneel on the rock, stare into the center of the sunflower and imagine my sister's beautiful face. "I love you, Jen Jen."

Beads drip down my face and I taste the salt on my lips as I watch the flower and my anger take their own journey, downstream, away from mine.

Graham's reassuring strokes unclench the knots in my back. He takes my hand, helps me to my feet, draws me into the shelter of his arms. He holds me like he'll never let me go. And even then, that would be too soon for me.

An inner calm prevails like I haven't felt since that not-so-normal Tuesday. We're all lost in our own thoughts, but as soon as we get to the edge of the stream, I break the stillness.

"One last squeeze?"

Marco reaches for my hand. Then like dominoes falling, I take Graham's, Graham reaches for Ben's, Ben grabs Jack's, Jack takes hold of Cass's. She closes the circle by grasping Marco's other hand.

My inner circle of amazing.

Chapter 25

Tuesday morning.

Truly just a normal Tuesday.

Graham and I meet up near the hammock. The grounds are strangely empty as we steal away to our special spot one last time before going our separate ways.

Graham kicks some fallen branches out of our path, juggling our faux picnic. I watched him like a hawk this morning as he took charge of breakfast. Carefully placing each breakfast burrito into the carry-away container, surrounding them with packets of salt, pepper and ketchup along with napkins so nothing would fall. Two coffees, one with extra vanilla creamer crammed tightly into the cup opening. White plastic lids pressed down to seal the heat inside.

Climbing down into the alcove, we move with ease into our customary positions, this time with a throw underneath us, cushioning our butts much better than the pine needles. He hands me a burrito but I wave him off.

"I'm not really hungry," I say.

Graham nods knowingly. "Me neither."

I take a sip of my coffee, nudging him in the ribs with my elbow. "Just the right amount of creamer."

"I know what you like," he says, all suggestive-like. And he's right.

"I'm glad we have a few minutes to be alone before our parents get here," I say.

"It's gonna be a bitch saying goodbye to everyone. You'll be the hardest."

"Stop with the puppy-dog eyes. It's not goodbye. It's *see you later*," I correct him.

"I know, but we won't 'see you later' until the end of August when I drive down. That's forever." He says this so earnestly I feel his angst and love.

I lean back, using my elbows to support my body. I have a clear view of my boyfriend.

Boyfriend. I like the way that sounds. Actually, I love the way that feels. "It's only a few weeks."

"Whatever, it's gonna blow."

Graham tugs on the corner of the throw, tossing it over the two of us, shielding us from the dampness of the morning. I sink into his eyes as my hands explore every inch of him, trying to memorize his feel on my fingers. I inch closer to him, wanting his body as close to me as humanly possible. He gently moves his hand under my shirt, then traces a heart on my stomach.

This guy.

I won't see him for another four weeks. Thirty-one lonely days. But I've weathered so much worse.

* * *

I zip up the last of the duffel bags. Even that sound is final. The room is pretty damn empty with Cass gone and the beds stripped. The butterflies in my stomach flutter around as I'm waiting to see my mom and dad. A text lets me know they're almost here.

I sit on the front step thinking about all I've been through in the last month. The gamut of emotions; the rollercoaster of feelings. None more comforting than the sight of my parents getting out of their car. I resist running toward them but I kinda want to.

They look so relaxed, their pace in sync. My God, they're holding hands.

As they get closer, I'm awestruck at what I see. No diamond earrings, no designer tie. My mom is wearing jeans and sandals and Dad is in a pair of cargo shorts and Top-Siders.

I can't wait anymore. I leap off the stairs and run into their arms. Screw being cool; I've really missed them. They wrap me up in a bone-crushing hug and I don't want to let go. When we finally unwrap ourselves, I ask: "Your clothes? What have you done with my parents?"

A much-needed laugh to stifle the teary reunion.

Dad says, "Let's start with the bad news, okay?"

My heart sinks. I can't take more bad news.

"Your mom and I signed us up for group counseling with other families who've been affected by suicide. It starts in a few weeks."

An entire summer of therapy. Good-feel killer. I don't know about this. After a month of grief camp?

Then Dad grins. "Before we tackle that, we planned a trip to Mexico. Make a new memory. We leave next week."

Note to self: get international plan for phone. Not seeing Graham is one thing. No communication: not going to happen.

My dad reaches over and rubs my head.

"You look great, Kai. Not just the hair."

We share the kind of laugh that we used to. Before we lost Jen. Before we lost our way.

When a glimmer of light at the end of the tunnel becomes a ray of hope, it's life changing.

Sandwiched between my mom and dad, hope washes over me.

I have them.

They have me.

Author's Note

I was writing an entirely different book when *Just a Normal Tuesday* was born. I was stuck and discouraged with my work in progress. So I did what writers do: I sent an email to another writer, Aaron Hartzler. As he was emailing me off the edge, he asked me if anything happened in my life when I was a teenager that affected the rest of my life. I wrote, "Well, my sister killed herself." I realized that I hadn't said those words out loud for many years. His response was simple and in all caps: THAT IS THE BOOK YOU HAVE TO WRITE. He told me this book would matter. Honestly, I wasn't sure I could do it. I knew if I did, I would risk exposing a secret that I had guarded for so long. I was embarrassed to say that my sister had chosen to kill herself. I felt as if people might judge me and her. I was afraid of the awkwardness that the word *suicide* brings to a conversation. So I simply went with the only-child explanation when anyone asked if I had siblings. It seemed easier than the alternative.

But the more I thought about it, I just couldn't shake it, so I started writing. I kept asking myself how my sister would feel about me doing this. That's when I found her suicide note, which I had hidden away long ago. In the note was my answer. Her final wish for me was that I embrace life and love what I do. That she would always watch over me. So I kept writing.

I wrote with the hope that some teenagers might see themselves on these pages and know they were normal. When I was a teen, I longed to see myself in a book. I didn't. So when the words were hard to write, I still kept writing.

One thing shared by every person who is left behind in the aftermath of a loved one's painful decision to end their life is the agony of wondering if there was anything you could have done to prevent it. The feeling of isolation can consume you because the truth is that no one can possibly know what you are going through unless the same thing happened to them. I wish that I had had a grief camp like the one in this book and the ones that are out there for teenagers now. I can't help but think it would have made a profound difference as at age fifteen I navigated the hardest thing I would ever face in my life. Grief camps are designed to guide you through the pain and bring a sense of normalcy back to your life.

In writing this, my adult self became my fifteen-year-old self in search of answers I would never find and I was forced to confront feelings I had buried. I didn't find answers but what I did find was forgiveness.

It is my hope that anyone who has suffered such a tragic loss will seek the help I didn't have. Writing this book freed me from the stigma suicide can bring. It provided me with a road map of forgiveness and allowed me to process my loss through a version of the grief camp I desperately needed at the age of fifteen. I wish my parents were alive so I could tell them that I finally realize that their loss was as enormous as mine.

Everyone in this world does the best they can. You never know what anyone else is going through. Things look bright and shiny on the outside but can be very dark on the inside. No one has a perfect life. Lead with kindness. Live your story. I chose the hashtag #liveyourstory for my book because your story is important. Living your life is important.

Every year tens of thousands of people commit suicide. In the United States, it's the third leading killer of kids between the ages of ten and twenty-four. In Canada, it's the second leading killer in the same age group. Go to http://toronto.cmha.ca/mental_health/ youth-and-suicide/#.V3aZVemzs6Y.

If you are struggling with thoughts of suicide, there is help.

Call the National Suicide Prevention Hotline, open 24/7, at 1-800-273-8255, or see http://www.suicidepreventionlifeline.org.

The Trevor Project has trained counselors to support you 24/7. If you are a young person in crisis, feeling suicidal or in need of a safe and judgment-free place to talk, call the Trevor Lifeline now at 1-866-488-7386.

The Hope Line is at https://www.thehopeline.com.

If you think someone you love is struggling, there's http:// www.helpguide.org/articles/suicide-prevention/suicide-prevention -helping-someone-who-is-suicidal.htm.

Your life is worth saving.

If you are someone who was left behind whether it be by a family member or friend who has committed suicide, died tragically or lost a battle with cancer or any other disease, there are incredible resources at camps like the Comfort Zone Camp (http://www.comfort zonecamp.org) in the United States and Camp Erin (http:// moyerfoundation.org/camps-programs/camp-erin/) in the U.S. and Canada.

Acknowledgments

I don't even know where to begin. Getting to this part of the book is overwhelming and all kinds of wonderful. This book was a lifetime in the making, so my emotions are all colliding.

Thank you to my agent, Bethany Buck. I could write an entire book about how thankful I am for you. Your unwavering passion for this story and belief in me was extraordinary. You were a cheerleader, a therapist and a champion. I will forever be gum on your shoe.

To my rock star editor, Kate Egan. The sequel to the above book would be all you. Your encouragement, compassion and mad editorial skills got me to the finish line. You are a dream to work with; I can't imagine this journey without you. Thank you for the gift of your magic touch with Kai, Jen and me.

To the team at KCP Loft: Lisa Lyons Johnston, Naseem Hrab, Michaela Cornell, Kate Patrick and DoEun Kwon. Thank you all for making my dream come true. I'm so proud to be part of this inaugural imprint.

A gigantic thanks to my amazing copy editor, Chandra Wohleber. Your eye to every tiny detail was epic.

So many thank-yous to designer Michel Vrana for capturing the heart and soul of my book with this cover. You're amazing.

Lin Oliver, thank you for opening up the world of children's book publishing to me by giving me the best job ever. And thanks to my SCBWI family.

Deborah Halverson, you read the very first draft and helped me shape this book into being submission-ready. Your talent and kindness were invaluable.

To Aaron Hartzler, there would be no book without you. A million thank-yous are not enough. I love you.

Tina Wexler, I am beyond grateful for you. You've been with me every step of the way and a few glasses of wine in between. I adore you.

A heartfelt thank-you to Martha Brockenbrough, Veronica Rossi and Sara Sargent, who talked me off the ledge when I was drowning in uncertainty and writer crazy. All of your texts, calls and check-ins got me through the toughest times. I love you all. I'm never giving you back.

Alessandra Balzer, Emma Dryden, Ellen Hopkins, Wendy Loggia, Krista Marino, Alex Penfold and Liz Szabla, I love having you all in my corner. You're the best.

Estelle Martinez and Michelle Miranda, thank you for making sure I got all the gory details right.

Mia Mantini, a million thanks for making me camera-ready and for the special place you have in my life.

Mary Bonanno, for being the greatest "nurse" and friend.

Sara Rutenberg, for guiding me through all the ups and downs. You were a lifesaver.

Thanks to Dan Mandel at Greenburger Associates for taking care of all the pesky details. It's much appreciated.

To my sorority sisters who became sisters to me. You know who you are. I'm so thankful you are still in my life. A special shout out to my "little sister" and college roommate, the only one who knew and kept my secret, Terrie Swopes, I love you.

To my inner circle of amazing:

Jenny Condon, the sister I would pick every time. Having you on my life team means everything to me. Your friendship grounds me. Thank you for being in the trenches with me while I navigated the rough waters and allowing me to turn the beach house into a writing retreat. Marlene King, my mentor and dear friend: All these years of your guidance pushed me to be the best I could be with every word. You are a treasure. Shari Rosenthal, thank you for reminding me that I could actually do this. LeeAnne Stables for being one of my biggest cheerleaders for so many years.

Kathie Calloway and Vicki McFadden, there are no words for all you mean to me. Erin O'Hagan and Laurie Semon, thank you for your friendship and making sure we didn't starve on the nights I couldn't leave the writer cave. Michele Carter and Cliff Todd, thank you for being family and never letting me give up. Sandee Forstall, my angel in heaven. I know you had a hand in this. I felt your presence with every draft.

To the family who lived through the aftermath with me at fifteen: Missy, Dean, Jackie, Stacey and lastly Paul, who my sister used to walk to school. Our connection will never be broken. Lucky me.

To the family who adopted me, the Smiths. Thanks for putting up with all the crazy that goes along with me and for understanding all the family events I had to miss while I was writing this book. I was there in spirit. I love you guys.

To my mother and father, who made me believe I could be anything I wanted to be. I did it. I wish you were here to see it.

I saved the best for last. To the person I could never have done this without, Bridget Smith. There were so many highs and lows during this process and you never wavered. You held my hand when things got rough and picked up all the pieces when I crumbled. You cheered me on when it all came together. You ate meals from cardboard containers, watched me pace the house in mismatched plaid, kept me stocked in snacks and loved me when I was swirling in some of the dark days writing this. You lifted me up with your smile and love. You are a beacon of positivity. I owe you all the everythings.

FAME. LOVE. FRIENDS. PICK ANY TWO.

MARIE POWELL
& JEFF NORTON

"You're the drummer," she said to herself. "It's your job to keep them on beat. To hold it all together."

But how the bloody hell was she supposed to do that?

KCP Loft

kcploft.com

DON'T MISS THE DEBUT NOVEL FROM WATTPAD SENSATION
DoNotMicrowave

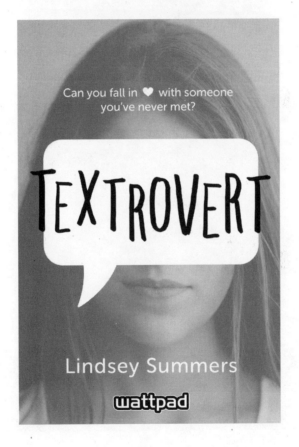

KCP Loft

kcploft.com

THE MORE I TOUCH SOMEONE, THE MORE I CAN SEE AND UNDERSTAND, AND THE MORE I THINK I CAN HELP.

What if one touch could tell you everything?

ZENN DIAGRAM

WENDY BRANT

BUT THAT'S MY MISTAKE. I CAN'T HELP. YOU CAN'T "FIX" PEOPLE LIKE YOU CAN SOLVE A MATH PROBLEM.

KCP Loft

kcploft.com